NATURAL CAUSES

Nan + Bill

NATURAL CAUSES
and other stories

Good Neighbors Bill

Gary McLouth

GARY McLOUTH

The Troy Book Makers
www.thetroybookmakers.com

The author may be contacted at:
Gary McLouth
c/o West Main Productions
P.O. Box 69
Slingerlands, NY 12159-9998

To order additional copies of this title, contact your local bookstore.
Or visit www.tbmbooks.com.

Cover photo of Dr. Sydney L. McLouth at 20 West Main,
Corfu, New York by Virginia Houseknecht McLouth.

Back cover photo by Russell Pierce.
Portrait of Gary McLouth by Providence Baker.

Cover and Book Design by Melissa Mykal Batalin.

Printed by The Troy Book Makers in Troy, NY on recycled, acid-free
paper. www.thetroybookmakers.com

ISBN-13: 978-1-933994-35-2

for

PROVIDENCE

CONTENTS

ACKNOWLEDGEMENTS

A WRITER stands on the foundations of his influences and experiences, no matter how disparate they may appear to critics, colleagues and friends. For me, there's Mr. Baim reading the seductive rhythms of T.S. Eliot in a creaking and hissing basement classroom in the Hall of Languages at Syracuse University; much earlier, silver, statuesque Martha Mansell reciting October's Bright Blue Weather in her fourth grade classroom at Corfu Central; the friendship of George Buggs in Oswego, Thom Edmondson in Kalamazoo, Marty Nakell in Albany, Chris Shaw in Lake Placid and Father Christopher DeGiovine at Saint Rose has counted when most needed. The graduate writing programs at Western Michigan University and SUNY Albany instructed and inspired, and William Kennedy and the New York State Writers Institute gave me the opportunity to engage writing and living writers in the present tense. I owe a sense of how stories resonate within a collection, across texts, and inside my self to Sherwood Anderson, John Gardner and Sue Miller.

The material of these stories has been challenging and at times threatening as layers of familiarity and fantasy peeled away to expose well protected truths. I wanted to focus particular attention on point of view and voice in order to establish the intimacy required by the characters while preserving the distance needed by the writer. Andrea Barrett in her advanced fiction workshop at Skidmore College's Summer Writers Institute provided essential criticism on two of the stories. Hollis Seamon gave me intriguing and helpful methods of approaching the family dynamics of experience and memory. I will be forever grateful for the guidance of these two fine writers and teachers.

We like to make such a big deal out of achievements like this humble set of stories, and, although I am proud of them, it's the business of living day to day that has dominated my time here. There may not be enough of the right words to say how much I've enjoyed the teaching-learning experience at The College of Saint Rose, but I can say for the gemutlichkeit generated by my students through the last 20 years, I am truly blessed.

FOREWORD

THE story goes that my father made a prenuptial proposal that my mother go to China with him on a medical missionary assignment during their first years of marriage. Personal circumstances, my mother's early bout with TB, children, a war-time, Genesee country practice and the verities of national politics responding to the communist takeover of China in 1947, grounded Dad and Mom in Corfu, New York, a village some 25 miles east of Buffalo and a long way from China.

There's an old Irish proverb that says the most beautiful music of all is the music of what happens. In a more contemporary version, John Lennon wrote that life is what happens while you're busy making (other) plans. That fit Dad's basic philosophy of life and he practiced medicine in much the same way, seamlessly planning while taking what came his way. He was good at what he did, and my mother was good at what she did, and together they lived a full life in Corfu, a life big as China and lots more fun.

Most of these stories germinated in the Corfu experience. Although times and places often reflect factual occurrences and situations, the characters, conversations, actions and themes are only as real as the human themes themselves. These stories are works of fiction. The inspiration for these stories is not. In the last year Mom and Dad lived together, they took me to Hooks, their favorite shoe store off Transit Road near Buffalo. I ended up with a pair of expensive and very comfortable sneakers. When I left Corfu the next day for Albany, Mom sang out the back porch door to remind me that the rhythm those sneakers would make on my walks went like: mom-dad-mom-dad. I swear I heard her voice call out the beat during the life of those sneakers. Mom(left)—Dad(right)—Mom(left)—Dad(right).

All writing makes sounds in the writer's head, and sometimes, vibrations resonate in the heart. Without language we would be imprisoned by the thrumming of the words wanting to get out. Sometimes the words themselves take to life and you have to measure and arrange them. I've found ways to direct this chaos, but I confess to a degree of simply hanging on until they've finished playing me. Robert Frost beckoned readers to go along with him on his poetic treks, as if he'd be alone without them. I'm surer than ever before that Frost knew he'd be both alone and with somebody the whole time. I may be sitting here 'alone' as I write these words, but I've got company too, and I hope you'll join us for awhile.

I'll tell you something train.
I no longer fear
that at night
you'll run so fast
through my mind
you'll shatter
the skull. I used to.
But I've built a railroad.
It has tracks as thin
and delicate as your first
purpose. As my own.
They are laid through the white
bone of my skull. They are yours,
train, to run on.

—from *Train* by Martin Nakell

VOICES ALONG THE ROAD

P EOPLE who aren't doctors will ask me, "What's it like to be a doctor, Doc?" and I probably don't satisfy 'em much with my little stories or simple quips like, 'it's great' or 'it beats a poke in the eye with a sharp stick' and so on. But what do they expect?

I know what they would ask if they knew how to ask it. They want to know about life and death. Because we all want to know, and it seems like I'd know something, having lost so damned many patients. That's what I think some of them think, too, without realizing it. How a guy like me presides over births and deaths without knowing. I just put on my kindly grin while wishing I could say, "you mean to say there's something to actually see?" I also wish I had a Lucky Strike to puff, and, I admit I wouldn't mind having an answer for the question.

We don't talk about it like that, like TV physicians with time on their hands as they sidle up to busty nurses taking poses at the ward station. It's what poets do, and what a few of us who wish we were poets try to get down in whatever

3

meager fashion. But none of my patients wonder about that. How I don't think about life and death even though I suppose it permeates my being; it's like thinking about blood types or heart valves. Try talking about those deep topics and watch the eyes glaze over. Few outside the field know or want to know how interesting those things are to me, but I understand.

One night not too long ago as I was driving into Batavia, I started thinking about how many times I'd driven that 14-mile stretch of road to the hospital. You take 45 years and multiply them by two or three round trips a day and you've stacked up some mileage. Then, the house calls. They're tough to figure, but within a 50-mile radius and an average of 100 to 150 calls a year, more in the early years, that adds up, too. It took me the whole drive in to get my formula, to categorize the routes and types of calls, the big ones being maternity cases and car accidents. On those you get the call and go. Fast. You're very focused, playing procedural routines in your mind and then preparing yourself for something you won't be prepared for. That's how I learned to do it at the old Syracuse Medical School, and it still works most of the time. Besides, it wouldn't be any fun if it turned out like the case studies and lab drills.

Over on the Colby Road one time, I got a call, rushed out of my office at two or so in the afternoon, waiting room full of patients, tore out there at eighty or eighty-five. I'm about to take the corner off Route 33, and there's this big crowd, cars lining both sides of the gravel road. We're out there in hay fields, mid-day, and there's a mob. I couldn't believe it. So, I have to park near the intersection, pull my black bag from behind the seat, and walk up the road. People were milling around, some were pushing forward and I fell in behind them for a ways. As we got closer I heard this wailing, a howl like a big wolf caught in a

4

trap. Then, people see me, you know, and the crowd separates. I walk down this human corridor in the middle of the country, never saw anything like it.

I zero in on a red truck. It's lying on its side. There's a crane attached to the flatbed and the crane is stretched across the road at an odd angle. A real mess, and the howling is clear as hell, now. The man is screaming a woman's name, and he's cursing God, and he's ranting 'motherfucker', which isn't the term of first resort around here. It's like he's holding the crowd at bay, screaming, but then a farmer runs up and tells me they've got a winch coming and they're going to pull the truck upright somehow. And, while he's promoting the plan to lift the truck, I'm trying to locate the screaming man.

That's the amazing thing to me now; no one said a word to me about the guy trapped in the truck. So, I sort of sashayed around the farmer and the pack of other guys kibitzing, and got myself right up to the truck. The cab is turned and bent, the driver's side is down but not quite flat against the gravel, and I get down on all fours and look in through the cracked windshield. He's big all right, and literally standing on his head, which I can't see from there, so I crawl flat and look around the crease near the back corner of the cab and there's his bloody, hairy head wedged perfectly between the door and the roof like a hardboiled egg in a nutcracker. One itty bit more pressure and the screaming would stop, pronto.

He was as scared as a man can be. He knew right where he was at. I heard the tractor pull up and men shouting directions at each other. One guy got a cable. Other men were running around the wreck, frantic to help out. Where I was, not three feet from the victim, my head was throbbing from the noise, but I had to get control of the situation. I knew that. I crawled out and stood in front of the wreck. I have no idea what I said exactly, but something to the effect of backing the hell off until

5

we got a calm, sensible approach to saving Red McNally's life. Oh, I'd gotten his name and a few other things out of him so I could get a line on his condition.

The troopers showed up, and when they saw me, they asked what I wanted them to do. The long and short of it is we got those crazy would-be rescuers organized, and I got back down on my belly to talk McNally down from his panic long enough to ask him what he wanted us to do. It was his life, after all. The truck was propped up by a big stone that had kicked loose from the ditch when he rolled over, and his head was pinched between the door and the frame. Snug, snug, snug, not one iota of space.

Anyway, McNally tells me his life story while we're under the wreck, me talking to the back of his head. He's been drinking for a week. Losing money. Punched his wife in the latest argument. His only son came home from Vietnam, arm blown off, on drugs now, down in Key West. And, he asks me: "Am I gonna die, Doc?" That damned question, and I'm scrunched as close as I can get, can't touch him or the truck, trying to keep him calm, all I can do is talk, and "am I gonna die, Doc?"

We got McNally's head out of the vise, I still don't know how we didn't crush him right there on the Colby Road. The cable held and the tractor lifted the wreck just enough to free him. A year later, McNally got himself killed good in a collision with a tree just past the Willow Bend Inn. DWI. On that one guy, I must have logged 60 miles by the time it played out. Two accidents, one coroner's case. Of course, he was included in hospital rounds for a few days. I could see the difference there between life and death physically. It was about this much the first time, and the second time, Ole Red left no margin of doubt. He had a panoply of injuries. The tree's alive and well today, put on fifteen feet and a cluster of new limbs.

You get to run your life by in little scenes and snippets while you're out driving between one thing and another. Maybe it's those moments that actually make life, the times of reflection in limbo. I hear my mother's admonition along the shoulder of the road sometimes. "Now, Benjamin, there's no reason why you won't become a doctor." How old was I when she said it first, almost in passing, not really to me at all but to her idea of who I would be when I'd be big enough to take up the course? Four, maybe? It wasn't long after that, my eyes started going bad. I can see the potato fields now, going misty and murky, like it was a low cloud day, rain closing us in. My father and the hired hand were out digging potatoes, and my mother brought me along with the lunch basket she'd made up for them. We went out from town in the Model A. Ma talked the whole way over the County Line Road, using only my full name, as she did, exclusively.

"Benjamin, are you listening?" That was Ma, always holding the attention of her class. She's the one who caught on that I wasn't seeing well. She gave me a couple of basic exams in the field that day and decided I would need glasses. Within a week she had me over to Doc Pierce's and into my first pair of a lifetime of glasses that ran from clunky horned rims to thin wire frames. I tried a monocle on my right eye, the bad one, in college. The frat boys loved it at the poker table. But my mother put the doctor strategy into motion early-on. I don't remember imagining anything else, except playing center field for the Yankees, blind as a bat. But it's a comfort to me now, hearing Ma's voice every once in awhile; it helps me to realize what I've become and how long it's been, and how short it seems, driving around in the Olds, getting around faster and in more comfort than in the old Model A, but still just getting around.

And maybe it's that woman's voice that kept me going

through the tough cases. I don't remember my father saying very much, but he sure was an excellent listener. Ma must have trained him before my brothers and I came along. "Now, Marshall," I could hear her start in as they went into the front bedroom upstairs down the hall from where I bunked with Jordie. "We'll get by this week on what we bring in from the stand and one of those leather necks scratching around in the side yard." After awhile, my father would say a couple of words, softly, and Ma would continue until you could hear Pa begin to snore. Then Ma would wind down and go to sleep.

I've gotten to be a listener, too, through years of disciplined training and habit. Being a doctor is about the business of complaint, really. If they're not complaining, they're most likely not looking for me. I'm lucky, I don't have many complaints myself, so I'm the ideal doctor, head like a fresh sponge. But I do have times of crisis and shock that shoot through me.

I got called on an accident over on Route 5 east of Pembroke near the Tonawanda bridge. It was a beautiful June night, a full canopy of stars, the crickets buzzing. The scene is lit up by the flares and red lights of fire trucks and state police cars which I can see from a mile away. Cars are pulled over, traffic rerouted. No matter how many car wrecks you see, they're always a surprise. Chaos. Everything turned in weird directions, broken glass, oil, pieces of cars strewn all over the place. And, at night, the spotlights and flares can disorient you.

I follow the parallel ruts off the road, down across the ditch, and into the edge of the field. There's a body covered by a tarp lying along beside what you wouldn't believe is a car. Only the right rear fender and taillight weren't smashed or flattened beyond recognition. The troopers and the Pembroke firemen are working the scene. A nice young trooper is showing me the ropes. "Here's the girl who was driving," he says, motioning to the tarp. "We think they got hit head-on by that Pontiac up there." I look up toward the road where a crew works on the twisted pile of junk. "There's one in there, too," the trooper says, so I'm thinking double fatalities, and I'm asking basic questions about speed, impact, identity, when I lift the corner of the tarp covering the girl, and I look into her face. She's got a laceration running high across her forehead, making a flap of skin that hangs over the bridge of her nose. It's clear that her chest is damaged. Compound fractures of both arms and severe leg injuries. I lift the flap of skin with my ballpoint pen; I'm squatting there in the flashing dark, and I recognize the girl. She belongs to the Bougereau family who used to live on the Dolge Road. I'd delivered this girl, sixteen, seventeen years before. The night suddenly got very cold, and when I stood, the stars were in my eyes.

The young trooper was still standing there, with a clipboard no less, and I swung my arm, it was a reflex I guess, and that clipboard sailed off into the dark. It shocked him, and before he could say anything, I pulled myself together. "Did you say 'they' officer? You mean, there's two people from this car?" And, he says, "we think so, Doc," and I do a couple of 360s to get my bearings and to get control of my temper, because now I realize there's somebody else out there who could be alive, and this guy is watching me look at a corpse. I try to reconstruct the accident from what little I've been told and gauge how far and in what direction another body could be thrown. This was before mandatory seat belts, you know. I start off into the high grass. There's a trio of firemen tromping around well west of my position, but I keep going on my criss-cross course, grass up to my waist, and just when I figure I've gone too far, I stumble on her. She moans not loud enough to hear beyond where I'm standing. I bend down; ragged breathing, rapid pulse, she's alive.

At the ER we're working like crazy to save the girl. She's banged up from head to toe. It's hard to imagine how thoroughly damaged a body can be and still survive. I knew we had a chance when her vital signs showed some stabilizing. We were afraid to use any general anesthesia, so she had to endure the pain of her injuries and the torture of our treatment, but she was one brave kid. If you believe in human bonding, it happened that night with all of us in the ER crew focused on one life together. It's exhilarating, I'm not ashamed to say.

Around two a.m., one of the nurses came in. I had an urgent call outside. Things were going as well as could be expected with our patient, so I stepped outside to take it, but there was no phone call. The anteroom was empty. I ducked out into the hall for a second to look around, and at the far end a couple sat against the wall. They got up and walked toward me. I must have been a sight in my blood-stained greens. I had my green cap on, maybe that didn't have blood on it, and as we came closer together, I recognize the woman. She's a little heavier in the middle, but her hair's jet black and she's wearing some kind of uniform. The man is tall, wispy thin, her husband. I haven't seen them for years, and I don't want to see them now. They walk up to me, faces bent in that horrible question mark, and I don't have a good answer to give.

He hits the floor with a smack. Mrs. Bougereau falls into my arms and clings to me, blood and all, in a death grip. No one had told them about their only daughter, and

I, being caught up in the moment of saving the accident's only survivor, had forgotten about Miss Bougereaus's parents, survivors of another kind. I held her until the shakes subsided, and until she was ready to let go. "She was all we have, Doc," she said.

Hospital hallways are well-lit, lonely places. I returned to the ER. Our patient would make it after a long, slow recovery and several corrective surgeries on her limbs and some serious plastic surgery around her eyes and mouth. I think she's married now, with children. Lives over near Elba. And, what about the Bougereaus, after all the years living and working in the area, raising Karen, their one child, caring for and loving her like I believe most parents do their children. I delivered baby Bougereau sixteen-and-a-half years before that night, assuming she would have a long, healthy life, saw mother and baby once or twice at the most, post delivery, and then, once again, the night she gets to drive home with a friend on her new night learner's permit. She's driving fine. The forty-one-year-old woman drunk returning to Niagara Falls from Batavia Downs isn't. They meet head-on.

I worry about Melanie, my youngest, and Barbara Ann, who doesn't drive all that well. How much I block their faces out of my mind so that I can pull back a tarp that covers a young girl's body. These miles I accumulate like some old warthog going about my mundane business. I know these roads too well, these solitary farmhouses and clustered bungalows standing in the night, their lone halogen lights bathing lawns, barn sides, and driveways in a kind of blood shadow. I picture my own village house, set back from the street, filled with the calm night breathing of my children, and my Marjorie. I listen to my mother's whispering in the rush of the roadside.

11

"So, I'm a doctor, Ma," I smile, content with the chill of the fading night.

"I'm not surprised, Benjamin," I hear her reply.

A woodchuck tumbles across my headlights for the other side of the road, and the wheels just miss him. With a little more luck we'll both be home by dawn.

THE FLORIDA ROOM

WHEN we returned from Easter vacation on Sanibel Island that year our backyard was barely free of snow, and the matted, wet leaves that we hadn't raked up in the fall clung to the bushes and lay around the base of the picket fence running along the western boundary of the property. We stood outside the back door, suitcases plopped on the steps while my father searched the glove compartment for the back door key.

"It's so ugly," Mother sighed, and I knew the vacation was officially over. As soon as dirty clothes from the trip were washed and put away we'd be raking, digging, planting.

"I want a Florida room," Mother said. "From the Florida room things won't be so ugly. Maybe we'll hear the ocean surf out beyond the trees," she said, with conviction.

"Ben," she turned to my father, who pinched the silver key between his thumb and forefinger. "Let's build a Florida room onto the back of the house; we should."

He didn't need to look her in the eye to verify her enthusiasm or her intention, even though I'm sure he thought of the obstructive location of the septic tank, or the magnitude of a project that would cut through the side of the house, violate the roof line and cost significant upheaval, to say nothing about money. He simply said, 'Okay'. Maybe it was easier than moving his practice to Fort Myers, which my mother and brother harped on all the way to the Blue Ridge Mountains until Dad lost his patience and told them to change the subject.

After waking Melanie from one of her deep, deep car naps, we unloaded, careful to deliver the conch shells and dried-out starfish the few final yards of the journey to the kitchen nook, a catch-all for everything in transition to someplace else. With that we were on our way to additions from Florida, the free kind.

• • •

My friend Beverly was having fun with boys the day after she passed from the womb to hear her tell it. By eighth grade she was very experienced and not too subtle about it, although she invariably prefaced and finished each tale of sexual intrigue with "promise not to tell a soul!" Her mother had a cousin who visited often from Grand Island. Beverly talked about her mother's cousin like she was royalty or somebody famous. Sometimes Cousin Louise brought her two sons along. It seems there was no husband, but Beverly never discussed that, even if asked. The little boy had some defect with his foot and Cousin Louise told rambling stories of their adventures at hospitals and clinics where specialists tried new techniques to make the boy's foot right. The older son was named Wayne. He was older than Beverly, but she wouldn't say how much older. Beverly's folks lived on a defunct farm on Lover's Lane over by the old apple groves that got cut in half by the Thruway. The low-built two-story house was set back from the road and a dirt driveway riddled with potholes ran between the house and the weathered barn set farther back closer to the Thruway. In the haymow of that barn, Beverly and Wayne did it.

To hear Beverly tell it you'd guess that Wayne was a sex maniac. He looked like Elvis, of course. Long black sideburns, slicked back DA. He curled his lips like Elvis did, swiveled his hips and never opened his eyes all the way except when he came, and then those big blues just wanted to roll down his cheeks in amazement. I never questioned Beverly's stories. Why would I? I enjoyed the Wayne stories, and unlike the other girls, I didn't repeat them. It wasn't so much that I agreed not to tell either. I got a special feeling, imagining Beverly and Elvis up in the haymow. It was exciting and creepy and bad and a little religious, too. I could also picture myself up there, and that was a secret I meant to keep.

•   •   •

Chase Martin was in the other section of our class in junior high and I noticed him during the breaks between classes when we passed in the hallways, more or less traveling in single file like good elephants on our way to the next 52 minutes of instruction by one of the half-dozen matriarchs and old maids whose lives I imagined to be composed of solitary suppers and grading homework. They were rigorous. Today, we'd call them focused, maybe obsessed. Chase Martin was taller than all but two of the other boys, and he already stooped like a farmer carrying the yoke. The farm boys all worked hard, but most of them left the obvious signs at home. The Martins, however, were not just farmers. My father liked to say they represent a unique time in American history. They were Jeffersonian, he said, and if you weren't careful, he'd go into a whole miniature lecture on what he learned at Hobart about Jefferson, Hamilton, and their competing visions for the emerging nation. I didn't see any resemblance to Thomas Jefferson in drooping, muscle-bound shoulders, but Chase Martin had stature, there was no doubt about that. He didn't like girls, so my friends said. He didn't talk to girls, he didn't look at girls. They said he didn't even think about girls, but who knew what he thought about?

When we passed in the dim high-ceilinged corridor making eye contact was difficult, but in the narrow stairwells, the snaking lines of students often brushed against one another. We could pass notes or swat books from each other's hands without getting caught. Between third and fourth periods on a Tuesday, I caught Chase Martin looking at me. I didn't exactly look away, but I didn't look him in the eye either. On Wednesday, we crossed glances. On Thursday, we definitely met eyes. On Friday, he was absent and fourth period American history before the Civil War lasted forever.

Sometimes before I fell asleep at night the crying of babies drifted up into my room at the back of the house. It was a long way from the examining room in my father's office, but the ducts for the old heating system were huge and resonant, and they carried the sounds when conditions were right. It was like I had a baby tucked under the wide window sill, the sound muffled as if she were lying face down in her pillow or wrapped too tightly in her blankie. I cooed in the dark sometimes to quiet her, and I felt something in my stomach like an easy cramping, a longing that would grow stronger from then on. I thought it had something to do with Chase Martin looking at me, and I've never fully decided since then it didn't.

A girl's life can be just so occupied with school, study, chores and hanging out with the girls. I wanted to go up into

Beverly's haymow to take a look around for myself, even though it was three weeks before Christmas and we'd had our first two snowstorms off Lake Erie. I called Beverly on Saturday morning and asked her what she was doing. I figured I could ride my bike out there and meet her around lunch, at which time her mother would be shopping in Batavia, and I'd be done folding the week's towels and bed sheets.

Riding my bike was a big mistake. The wind cutting across Cemetery Hill went right through my wool jacket. The shoulder of Allegheny road was frozen into ruts and I had to steer along the edge of the pavement and lean against the wind too. I got to Lover's Lane exhausted. Beverly gawked through the kitchen window at me and opened the door.

"Your face is on fire," she announced.

"No shit, Sherlock," I croaked.

Beverly went to the sink and ran warm water into a clean dish towel. "Poor baby," she cooed and patted my face. "Too bad we don't have a fireplace to huddle up to, B.A., but the space heater is just as good." She took my jacket, which felt like an icy skin being peeled off me, and we sat on stools next to the big heater jutting out from the inside wall of the kitchen. Bright sunlight poured through the rear windows facing the barn. Farther back, cars glinted by on the Thruway.

"So, watcha up to today, B.A.? There's a new Elvis movie out, you know."

"This is it for me, Bev. I think I'm going to glue myself to your stove until my bones thaw out. Then I'm donating that old bike to the Catholic church rummage sale. After that, a cab would be nice."

"Wouldn't it be great to have taxis out here!" Beverly screamed in excitement. "I love those yellow cabs with the

19

black lettering, don't you? The big, boxy ones you see pulling up at the Waldorf Astoria."

"In your dreams!" I made a wide open, gums exposed grin.

"Taxi! Oh, taxi, puh-leeze." Beverly lifted her leg and mocked my grin.

"I can just imagine a cab pulling into the driveway out here. How weird could you get, huh?"

"Too, too. It would be great, but I don't know, B.A., nothing would be the same again, so maybe it's a good thing it won't happen."

"Oh, come on, that's just what we need," I said, half-serious.

"I called one, you know."

"What!"

"Yeah, I called a taxi from the Yellow Pages. We have a Buffalo phone book. The dispatcher asked for my address, and when I told him, he laughed at me and said he couldn't send a cab until we had streets out here. Do you believe that? 'Asshole,' that's what I should have called him. The line went dead too quick."

I leaned against the stove. The grill was so hot, I flinched. It occurred to me how fires started in the winter inside these uninsulated houses with their space heaters cranked up against the cold.

"Want something to eat? We've got tuna salad left over from last night, and my Mom made bread this morning. It's still warm."

"Sounds great to me." I loved home-baked bread. I liked milk fresh from the cow too, almost anyway. My mother always warned us kids about unpasteurized milk. Her best girlfriend in high school had died of undulant fever. Mom kept a snapshot of her in the lower corner of her dressing table mirror.

Beverly moved around the kitchen like a pro. She plunked the thin china plate down on the porcelain laminated table and set a tall glass of Neelands Dairy milk alongside. The milk wasn't homogenized so the cream floated to the top and made scum around the rim, like white lipstick.

"This looks so good, Bev, you should be a chef, or a waitress, at least."

"I'd rather own the place, but I'll be lucky to waitress," she laughed.

The tuna sandwich was saturated with mayonnaise and oil, and it ran down my fingers and wrists. Beverly handed me a napkin. "First-rate service," I nodded, and put the sandwich back on the plate so I could wipe my hands. I spotted the waste basket in the corner next to the sink and thought about tossing the wadded napkin over there. I was good in intramural basketball, and I was sure I could hit it. Then Beverly's eyes widened and her shoulders squared, tense like the cords in her neck. "Oh, my God," she whispered.

I turned halfway around in my chair to see what Beverly was seeing. A dark blue two-door Chevy bounced up the driveway. It was dented in the left fender behind the headlight. The car stopped just short of the back door where my bike leaned against the side of the landing. When the woman got out of the driver's side, the wind beat her frizzy hair forward around her face. The boy bundled in the red snowsuit and hood hobbled from the other side of the car; his leg brace glinted in the cold sun. The other boy got out last, and I was already looking for the sideburns, the pouting Elvis lips, maybe a twitch in his hips as he walked across the uneven driveway. But he wasn't much bigger than the first boy. The wind whipped his light-colored hair and he raised his hand to sweep his angled bangs back into the right direction, a futile effort. I heard Cousin Louise urge them to move faster to the house, and when the Elvis one looked up into the window's glassy reflection, I was sure he couldn't be over twelve. "Don't you tell a soul, B.A.," Beverly cursed as she skipped by me to the door, "please."

•   •   •

During Christmas vacation the Martin family held their annual sledding and skating party. It was an all-day outing that started in mid-morning with the boys playing tackle football in the Martin's barnyard. The game went until noon, when they would be thoroughly covered in mud and manure and their overalls were ripped and torn. No girls were allowed to come in the morning, and by the time we arrived between one and two, the boys were cleaned up like country gentlemen. They had also shoveled the snow from the pond and cut toboggan runs down the steep pasture slope that ran along the ridge made by the glacier and Lake Ontario a long time ago. It was the first year I received an invitation from Mrs. Martin, who established the rules and programs for the outing. You had to be at least in junior high school, and you had to be a classmate of one of the five Martin children. Since they were spaced every two to three years, that meant a lot of kids, and Chase being the fourth Martin child meant that my first outing was heavily attended. I was in the fledgling flock, as Mrs. Martin called us. I would be a fledgling.

From the logs surrounding the crackling bonfire by the pond you could keep half-warm while watching the furrows of snow flying like smoke behind the toboggans hurtling down the ridge. You can't really steer a toboggan by leaning like they tell you to do, and from far off you can see that it's like riding a rocket. You went fast in the direction you set from the start. Fast, and straight down.

The girls got to scuffle around on the ice like drunken mice. Mrs. Martin set up a plank table where she kept the hot cinnamon cider and warm sugar donuts in double boiler pans she heated in the milk house of the main barn. The barn rose a tall three stories to a steep roof, and the cupola perched at the exact center of the roof beam was red, trimmed in white. The weather vane turned noiselessly in the light wind, and I wondered who climbed up there to oil and paint the proud brass Holstein cow.

Mrs. Martin skate-danced. She and Mrs. Barthoff and Mrs. Seirk formed a line and skated backwards in a slow arc around the ice. They laughed and talked as if they weren't even thinking about falling. Mrs. Martin had strong legs, and when she anchored the turns she dug in smoothly, her blades wafting up ice chips like a spray of baby powder.

A few of the boys came down from the ridge to get warm around the fire, and a couple of the older boys laced up hockey skates and charged around the pond like circus bears. Chase came down later and stoked the fire from the scrap lumber piled against the corner of the milk house. I watched him carefully loop the laces of his skates into double-bow knots. His fingers looked absolutely frozen. Then he got up and skated smoothly over to where I sat to ask if I wanted to skate. It was the first time he ever spoke directly to me. When he noticed that my ankles buckled like butter, Chase decided he should show me the barn.

Inside the Martin's big barn I felt like I'd entered a huge Egyptian tomb. From the plank floor to the roof beam a series of wooden rungs ran an uneven vertical ladder across the butt ends of a thousand bales of hay. The only light cracked in between the long vertical boards of the wall, and when my eyes got adjusted the low-ceilinged stalls and bins, where tools and equipment were kept, lined the other side of the wide, chaff covered floor. Above the stalls another series of haymows rose to the pitched roof, but they were only partially full and unevenly stacked so that after climbing the first short set of rungs beveled into the beams near the grain bins, you could climb the tiers of hay bales like you were traversing a cliff. There were holes to watch out for, and pigeon nests in the eves, and you could hear the birds gargle softly as if reporting our progress to each other. I had heard stories at school about the corn-cob wars the farm kids fought in their barns. In my imagination these so-called wars were nothing more than a few harmless pieces of corn being tossed around, but up here the immensity overwhelmed that impression. The sides of the bales were sharp enough to chafe your legs right through your pants. Trap doors and sheer walls made fast movement tricky. You could break your leg, fall like a stone through a hidden shaft. I saw that it was hard field corn cobs they threw at each other and it was easy to imagine the heavy artillery of those cobs when loaded with the pebble-like kernels of field corn.

Chase was proud of the barn. He told me how many bales they could load in a day, what the weight of the mow, fully loaded, would be in kilograms. I forgot the numbers immediately. His voice had a hollow sound in the big bell of the upper mow, and as I sat on the overlook made by a ledge of bales, I imagined falling, looking through the dusty light that would whisk by on the way down to the hay-padded floor. "We're up about 25 feet," Chase said. "In July, we wouldn't be able to sit here."

"Oh," I sounded airy to myself.

"Nope, there's fifty-pound bales stacked all the way to the track." He pointed at a single rail mounted below the roof beams. It ran from the square peak windows all the way across to the other mow, where it disappeared above the hay.

"Gee," I said.

"I'm getting hungry, are you ready for the roast, Barbara Ann?"

It was the way he said my name, very carefully, almost tentative as if he were about to lift a glass-blown figurine to see how the light would color it. My legs felt weightless as we climbed down. I was sure my foot wouldn't find the next rung all the way down. It was so natural for Chase to show me the barn. I could have been anybody and he'd have taken her to the same places, said the same things, except that 'Barbara Ann'.

•   •   •

I lay on my bed, radio low on WKBW. "Love Letters in the Sand" took me back to the beach on Sanibel Island. Through my window the snow fell thick and soft in that way it has when there's no wind. Although we were moving up on New Year's Eve, no special plans were made. Oh, we'd go to Aunt Lorraine's. We didn't need an invitation for that. Dad would get a maternity call around ten. Maybe he'd be the lucky doctor to deliver the New Year's baby. "Girls, Girls, Girls Were Made to Love" finally shut Dick Biondi up for a couple of minutes. A stupid song, but then, Elvis. Teddy bears, and bees buzzing. Uh,uh,uh-huh. He was truly stupid, but my foot was going with the beat under the corner of the quilt.

I wondered what Beverly was doing now that school was out and it was snowing every day. It must be frigid out in her barn, so small compared to the Martins' that it could be swallowed whole by one hayloft alone. I pictured Wayne's fuzzy cheeks and Beverly pushing him down into a hole between the rows of bales because he couldn't grow sideburns. Then Nat King Cole cut in. "Love is a Many

Splendored Thing." He sang as if he really meant it. There was no buzzing and humping, and I felt the undertones I wouldn't understand until later. Then, I laughed, picturing Wayne's baby face flushed in the buzzing of Beverly's mow. Mom knocked on my door and popped her head in. I was sprawled out, laughing; I couldn't stop.

"What in the world is so funny, dear, you're in hysterics!"

"Mom, tell me, is love a many splendored thing?!" I laughed a pitch higher, tears in my eyes. She came in and sat on the bed. "Oh, my," she said, and began laughing too, although more like Nat King Cole might laugh, thoughtfully.

After the Christmas recess, Chase Martin and I "dated" a little, went to the movies at Dipson's in Batavia a couple of Friday nights with a carload of friends. His mother drove once, and my mother drove the other time. I felt light-headed, pressed against his hard body, five of us crammed into the back seat of the station wagon, everybody talking at once. Riding in the cold moonlight, compacted, going along those strangely familiar roads was such a carefree feeling. I wondered what it would be like, driving with Chase alone, talking with just him in the car, in the moonlight.

Since Chase played basketball on the junior varsity, I got to see a lot of him in his shorts and jersey. Basketball season ended right before Easter when the Martin family took their one annual out-of-town vacation, and upon their return from Myrtle Beach or Daytona, the outdoor work began in earnest. Chase's time for after-school sports or study clubs evaporated, along with our "dating" time to sit around the cafeteria with our friends. Years could pass like that, I remember thinking at the wise old age of fifteen. Seasons of plowing, planting, cultivating and harvesting interwoven with Halloween, the Martin family outing and basketball. I marked my wall calendar with a code of symbols devised for keeping track of my splendored thing with Chase. The circle with the 'X' inside showed Friday nights or Saturday afternoons when no family commitments or games were scheduled, when his mother or my mother had the car, and the time. If 'rare' was synonymous with 'splendored,' then I was sittin' on top of the world with two years' worth of precious, crossed circles.

•   •   •

The basketball season of our junior year was as precious as my moments with Chase Martin. The varsity won all its games but one, and we were playing Leroy, our lone conqueror, in their gym on the Friday night after Washington's birthday. Chase was still hurting from a shot he'd taken under the basket in the previous game against Attica, and he couldn't lift his left arm above chest level. He hadn't played much in the Leroy game. In the fourth quarter Leroy led by six points and seemed ready to ice the game with their best shooter standing at the foul line waiting for the ball from the referee. You could hear a feather float it was so quiet. Our cheerleaders were on their knees near the players on the bleachers. You could almost see the ball swishing the net, but before it happened, our coach called time out. Our group of loyal fans cheered in relief. The team huddled around the coach, and when they went back onto the floor Chase was with them, lining up under the basket. The Leroy shooter missed the shot, Chase blocked out underneath, snared the rebound with his good hand and rifled a long outlet pass on the fast break, a quick two points. He then batted Leroy's inbounds pass to our guard for a layup, another fast two points. Down by one basket, our defense dropped back and when Chase rebounded the next missed shot, their big center grabbed him by the left arm and swung Chase against the pads under the basket. Chase howled and grabbed his wounded wing. I leaped to my feet, crying out myself, wounded too, the pain in his shoulder transmitted directly to my heart. In those few seconds in the Leroy gym on a cold February night, I was as close to another human being outside the family as I'd ever felt. They let Chase shoot his foul shots even though he couldn't balance the ball with his left hand. He missed the second one, and Leroy won by that point. Chase was taken straight to the hospital. I cried all the way home.

The Florida room warms in the early spring sun so that you feel summery long before green returns to the lawn, long before the buds on the maple trees redden. Mom grew Norwegian pines in big tile pots out there, and kept a tray of geraniums alive all winter for their vibrant color and heavy scent that reminded all of us of June. But it was usually too cool to sit for long, and the Florida room was as much an idea as it was a place to go, so I was using it as my own private refuge. The day after the game I woke late and didn't go downstairs for breakfast or lunch. Mother brought me toast and tea around ten, but left to do the weekend shopping. Dad held morning office hours and left for the hospitals. I knew the sounds and movements below me, listened for the tuneful conversations. My brother was never in the house on Saturday, and my sister Melanie was the miniature opposite-sex model of my brother, never enough action to get into. I loved my lonely days in the house, in my room. The hallways could be adventuresome, and I often waited for those special times when I was the sole surviving Wells, so-to-speak, when I could go from room to room and just be filled up on the quirky life in each of them. Barefoot,

I went down the back stairs. Bright sunshine criss-crossed the kitchen floor and I visualized the beach for a moment, how nice it would be to lie on a blanket among the shells, listening to the soft surf, with Chase. The heat would heal his arm, and we could kiss.

The Florida room annex was certainly as beautiful as Mom had planned, but it was also as problematic as Dad had cautioned. The roofing job hadn't been done quite right, and the ice buildup sprung leaks along the joint between the old and new construction. Mom draped old curtains over the imported teak-framed glass doors to protect them and put buckets along the doorway to catch water. Instead of opening the low-ceilinged family room to the glorious light coming through the wide window of the Florida room, the curtains made it darker than ever, and I couldn't see into the Florida room until I was nearly standing in the doorway, like a statue.

Mother lay back on the chaise. Dad straddled her, a quilt draped over his back, his head bent forward. She arched at an odd angle and her head turned to the side facing me, her eyes closed, her long, swanny neck throbbing. She made a faint singing sound of one long note, and then her eyes opened, blankly for a moment before she made a big round 'GO' with her mouth, and I did, stealing away with a picture that fit the words I'd been carrying around in my head, feeling the terrible thrills of sex and guilt in my stomach. I knew this new secret would be my mother's and mine alone, and that I wanted to go all the way. I would even tell her so.

•   •   •

Chase got the cast off his arm in time for the May Fest held on the school football field. It was set up like a miniature firemen's picnic with booths for skill games and handicraft displays. Our teachers manned the barbeque pit where they turned whole chickens and one piglet, all donated by the Martin family farm. Cold pop and hot dogs, cotton candy, caramel corn and ice cream came from the super market. Candied apples on sticks were made by the Women for a Better Town of Pembroke. We had it all. Chase walked me around, favoring his weak shoulder. I remember kidding him about being a wounded duck and poking my brand new polished finger nails into his ribs. He put his good arm easily around me and grinned his big-toothed, cowboy grin. It was neat, because we never really talked much, not even on the phone. I remember a lot of conversations that went on in my head. Perfect.

When Mrs. Martin called that Memorial Day weekend to see if Chase had stopped by our house, I assumed as she did that he'd taken their car out for a spin with his newly minted driver's license. He'd inexplicably flunked the road test the first time and seemed vindicated at passing it the second time with a 95 percent rating. Mrs. Martin asked to speak with my mother, and I handed Mom the phone and went out into the yard. We were supposed to take a three-day weekend up to the Adirondacks, but Dad was still on maternity at the hospital and we now had only two days off and if he wasn't back by noon, I was sure he'd cancel the trip. I had hoped Chase could come with us. I begged Mom to invite him, and she gave me that look: where would he sleep? The cabin's two bedrooms were joined by a wall that stopped short of the ceiling. I knew what she was thinking. I'd find a way to make love with Chase while my brother and sister slept next to me and she and Dad snored away on the other side of the stupid wall. I gave in to the sudden flush of anger and betrayal I felt, almost blasting the "F" word in her face, but I ran up to my room instead.

The apple tree was in full bloom, and I stood under its bonnet of white lace. Bees buzzed, birds sang, the lawn grew thick and green. Dad did return by noon, and he honked the horn as he pulled up to the back gate at the head of the driveway. We would go to the mountains after all.

The lake was crystal clear and nearly as cold as the winter ice which had held the surface up until three weeks before. We swam anyway; it was exhilarating beyond belief. I lost my burn towards Mother in that water, and she didn't mention a word about it until we passed the Canandaigua exit on the Thruway on the return trip.

"Well, I wonder if Ole Chase has returned home with the Martin family farm wagon," she sang, half-kidding. I'll never forget the way she said 'Ole Chase' as if he were a forgetful old man who'd wandered off. When we got home, there was a note pinned on our screen door. I caught Mr. Martin's signature on it before Dad took it down, read it, and handed it to my mother. "Well, I wonder," she sighed, and left her suitcase at the door to go to the phone.

I thought I had a lot of friends, but curiously, after Chase disappeared, they were inflicted with amnesia like Bette Davis in a black and white movie. 'Oh, Barbara Ann', eyes looked through me, voices passed by me. Only Beverly acted normal, and she was never really normal. Chase had run away, driven away, in fact. Alicia Severance was gone from her parents' ranch house on the Cohocton Road. Missing since the day before Memorial Day. Both of them.

What did I know about this, I was asked a hundred times. The Martins, the principal, the New York State Police. A week went by and then two, three. At graduation, the junior class sat in the front section of the school auditorium vacated by the senior class now on stage, having moved up from the back rows since the seventh grade. Two seats were left vacant in the second row where Chase and Alicia might have sat. It was dreadful sitting in that section. And, it was hokey. The whole ceremony was haunted by the two empty seats.

•   •   •

I spent many days with Beverly that summer. Her mother worked at a new job in the Batavia knitting mill as a manager, and her father still drove long-distance truck. There was enormous time to kill. From the broken double doors that hung open from the back of their decrepit haymow, Beverly and I counted cars, trucks, motorcycles, police cruisers, boat trailers, moving vans. We recited Regents questions we'd missed, and the bra sizes of every girl either of us had ever seen in the locker room. We talked about the black mustache that made Miss Chit look like Zorro, and the skinny shoulders that cast Mr. Donahue as Mr. Peepers. Beverly brought the transistor Motorola up, and we sang with everybody but Frank Sinatra, who neither of us trusted a moment with his black magic stuff—"he'd have your panties down in a minute"—Beverly gushed. "wouldn't look at your face, know your name, nothing', just a slick screw." That made me laugh, always.

We had quiet times too, just watching traffic pass. When it rained, the trucks trailed huge clouds behind them and you could see the cars following blind, going fast, going blind. I wondered where Chase was. Why he'd gone. Why he'd gone with Alicia Severance, who no one knew, and who Chase had just met, if even that. I was stuck on an endless toboggan ride. I couldn't stop thinking about what I'd done or didn't do. Alicia Severance was a mask.

My mother came into my hot, stuffy room at night. She knew I was in there, light off, eyes half-closed, half-open, waiting it out.

"It'll be all right, honey," she assured me. "There's lots to be thankful for. It could be you lost out there someplace. We'd be just as devastated as the Martins are. We're glad you're home."

I knew this to be true, and I would squeeze Mother's hand to let her know. But I also wanted to be wherever Chase was, out there, to rub his sore shoulder, to talk about what he was thinking about, to make love. My stomach wouldn't ache, I thought, and maybe things would be splendored, like in the Florida room.

IN THE GAME

W E were sitting around the big round oak table in the dining room waiting for the water to boil for my brother's latest gift to Mom, an antique Crosley drip pot he picked up at the flea market in Zenia, Ohio, on his way back from Kalamazoo. He'd met Brian Barnes out there at a fiction workshop. Brian was crossing the country on a book tour, and since he and my brother Danny hit it off so well, he decided to ride through with him on his way east. Brian didn't have any readings scheduled between Michigan and Schenectady, where he said he planned to stay with his first ex-wife's sister.

Sunday afternoon dinner spanned its usual pattern of interruption even though it began in routine fashion. Dad sliced the London broil into thin strips the thickness of South Carolina bacon while Mom rushed the scalloped potatoes dish into the dining room by the sheer will of one ragged pot holder which burned through to her hands midway to the table.

"Oh-my-God," her eyes teared up, she shook her hands violently and returned to the kitchen to rescue garlic Italian bread from the smoking oven. "Where's the salad," she yelled to no one in particular. She found it already tossed and chilling on the back porch where she put it an hour before.

"Thought we'd have to substitute sliced carrots," she said, relieved. "Light the Sterno under the bean dish, will you, Mel? We'll be ready in a jiff." A jiff usually meant anywhere from between the next incoming call and the charring of today's forgotten oven dish, but the food hit the table in sync, and after Brian and my brother came in from their fireside chat of poetry and baseball in the living room, Dad reached out with both hands to urge us into a circle around the table. Taking my mother's hand to his left and my brother's to his right, Dad nodded and lowered his head. Grace ended with a reminder to God and to whoever else might be listening that we were all in this game together, that we had to be loving and patient with each other, even when it appeared in our best interests not to be, even as we would judge others instead of judging ourselves. For Brian Barnes my father asked a special blessing, for his calling to the language of our hearts. My mother raised her eyes a beat before the amens. I could tell she'd sniffed out Barnes' calling already, and sometimes I wish I'd been as good a bloodhound, even at that precocious age.

Brian sat on my left. For his first move he slathered a gob of butter on my bread plate. He then spun the lazy Susan to reach the hot garlic loaf swaddled in bright red cloth and quilted foil. The serving spoons spun free and clattered in front of mother's setting. Danny caught the pepper mill, fine second baseman that he'd been in high school.

"I hunger for the bread of life," Brian drawled in an accent grinding Kentucky and the Simi Valley horrendously together. "Or is it the life of bread I so hunger to devour!" He let out a whoop and clapped my father on the upper arm. Then he drank water from Dad's stemmed crystal with his left hand. So far, he had not touched any of his own dishes or silverware, and I wondered if he were taking pre-emptive action to nullify my father and me as competition for the London broil that escaped centrifugal force by sitting in the center of the lazy Susan.

Mom outstretched him quickly by retrieving the serving spoons and asking for his plate, serving ample helpings of scalloped potatoes, boiled carrots (she cooked them "just in case") and applesauce with chutney. Then she held the plate out toward father, and he neatly layered the open quadrant of the blue Wedgwood plate design with fine, juicy strips of pink meat.

"Thank you, doctor, it's a real pleasure for me to be here, you're lovely folks, lovely indeed."

My father's face broke into delightful confusion. "You have a way with the words, Mister Barnes."

Brian helped himself to the Merlot from the carafe mother had unearthed from the cellar "antique" room and poured a brimming portion into my wine glass without looking at me or asking if I wanted any.

"That's a lot for me," I whispered.

"You!" He jerked sideways to look me in the eye. "How lucky can you get, sitting next to a generous scoundrel like me. You could suffice for weeks on end by simply hanging around the edges of any table I chose to sup!" He laughed uproariously and threw his head back as if punched in the nose by Smokin' Joe Frazier. My mother laughed too, and shot Danny the look that said: *you've rounded up another lunatic to entertain and pillage us.*

Brian Barnes would eat the whole table and all of us around it, or so it felt like, sitting next to him, flinching in anticipation of the thrown hand, the percolating body language.

"Deconstruction is taking over the genre," he pronounced, wolfing Mom's scalloped potatoes. "How do you transform ugly groundlings into such joie de palate, Missus Wells—god, I'd uv driven all the way 'cross Georgia on a three-legged mule for just one spoonful."

"Well," my mother countered with good manners, "you've ridden across the Ohio, Pennsylvania and New York State turnpikes, and that's enough to make a man hungry."

"No, Missus Wells, a man starve or a starving man." He beamed at Mom across the table until her face shone as pink as his. "Ben, please give Brian more steak," she surrendered.

"How about the beans, Mother?" My brother loved the way she made the long string beans and mushrooms in light cream sauce, heated to just short of curdling in a copper pan over Sterno. I thought she'd forgotten to mention it intentionally so Danny would have to inquire and then pay tribute to the recipe and her way with cooking. At least, that's how it happened each time she made them when Danny came home.

"Wait till you taste the beans, Brian, you won't fucking believe it!"

My father looked up at Danny and winced. No one said the *F* word in any of its forms inside the house, although Dad blurted it out once when we turtled the canoe up at the lake. I never looked at Mom when my brother offended her. It was too much disappointment to bear. Brian, naturally, read the signals conversely.

"Fuckin' A-yup," he croaked. "Hey, after you been havin' steak for a long time, beans, beans, taste fine. And, after you been drinkin' champagne and brandy, you're gonna settle for wine! Kingston Trio, fifty-eight, fifty-nine!"

I couldn't believe he was such a jerk. Mom procured another loaf of steaming hot garlic bread as a complete surprise to all but Brian who seemed to be expecting it. "Oh,

Missuzzzz Wells! Wonderful!" He ripped off the end pieces and stuffed them into his mouth, one after the other. The carafe stood empty near the corner of his place mat until he ceremoniously plunked it onto the lazy Susan, shoving the carrot dish into the steak plate which nudged the salt shaker over the edge onto my plate, a billiard shot that defied the probabilities of physics.

"It's a true, true privilege to find a table like this in the post-modern world," Brian said in the clearest, unaffected accent you've ever heard. "It's a pleasure to be here, doctor." He toasted my father with his water glass, whereupon Mother jumped up to refill the carafe in the kitchen. Dad nodded and chuckled, and I thought about how my family seemed to be a magnet for oddballs.

The wine looked regal as the light refracted through the deep red liquid in the carafe. It should be left full and set in the center of the table always, I thought, as a symbol of our family's good spirit, and as a link to the kind of communion I felt with the world in general, even if people like Brian Barnes took advantage of us in a way, but he was also the kind of person who made life interesting, so things sort of evened out.

Only my brother had gotten up to help himself to the beans and mushroom dish, and he was sipping the last of the milky broth from his spoon when the doorbell made its two-note call. "Doorbell," Danny sang.

"I'll get it," my father got up, laying a hand on Brian's shoulder. "Please excuse me, Brian, Sundays schedule themselves around here. I'll be right back."

I loved the way Dad made smooth exits from dinner or supper, always expecting the call, but never betraying a sense of expectation or acting resentful of having his time taken. Graceful, he was.

"We'll miss you, doctor." Brian filled his glass and tippled enough Merlot into mine to swell it to the brim. I felt he'd stolen a personal accomplishment right before my eyes. I'd never finished one of mother's goblets filled with wine before, not even at Christmas. "Bottoms up," Brian raised his glass and his thick eyebrows in unison. Mom caught my eyes quickly. She didn't want another sip of that Merlot going down her teenaged daughter's throat. In fact, when she got up from her chair, I thought she was coming to take my glass away. The first wine must have made me a little paranoid because she would never embarrass me in front of guests, not that Brian was a guest any longer or that he would have noticed a damned thing. No, she'd gone to check the driveway from the living room window. "Oh, darn," I heard her say to no one in particular. "Another Sunday, ruined."

"Marj!" My father called from the office. He recruited her to fill in on weekends when the nurses were off and he had patients backed up, or there was a fractured arm to support while he set the bone and wrapped the splint or layered a plaster cast. She apologized with an air of relief for her sudden departure and walked quickly through the double Dutch doors into the office out front. Then, Danny got up to look out the front windows. "Emergencies jazz people, Brian," he said excitedly when he returned to the table.

"Yeah, you can see what people are made of when the heat's on. Panic is a mad dog right below the surface, and you have to temper it, or it'll eat your face off," Brian recited around a mouthful of food.

"Let's go see what the doc's life in small town America is all about!" Danny relished the chance to share some real turf with Brian. But after digesting so much of Brian in such a short period of time, I wondered how Danny had survived a day and night hunkered in the Volkswagen with him. Brian gobbled his steak cud and gulped half a glass of wine. "Blood and guts, yeah," he blurped.

•   •   •

The village ambulance and the fire department's rescue van sat nose to tail in the lower driveway. Half a dozen volunteer firemen and the ambulance drivers milled around the vehicles. A misty rain webbed the low sweeping pines. The wipers of the rescue van swapped back and forth.

My brother and Brian were out in the rain with them. Danny knew the guys from high school and the local gin mills where he hung out on breaks from college and the quilt of jobs that followed. That was my brother, had to know everybody in the room, in the town, in the world. When he played baseball, he would have everyone in the bleachers classified into two groups by the third inning: those he knew and those he was going to know. Playoff games could take him into the fifth inning. The championships that one year in Rochester finally undid him with ten thousand fans. He couldn't single people out and play the game too. "They knew my number," he said, sarcastically, from the back seat of the Oldsmobile on the way home. He struck out three times and booted a double-play grounder. Dad told Mom and me, while Danny used the restroom at a gas station, that if Danny had kept his eyes on the 'damned ball' instead of peeking into the stands, he'd have made the play when it counted. I watched Danny come around the corner of the Sunoco station. His head was down, but he was smiling in that introverted twist he has on himself. Instead of getting back into the car, he ambled over to my father's side and leaned through the open window, his face a foot from Dad's.

"Were you telling them how that chewed-up infield steered the DP ball off my glove?"

"You had it all the way, Danny," Dad said without hesitation. "The breaks of the game."

Danny patted Dad's shoulder and walked around the rear of the car and got in next to me. "I knew you knew I had it, Dad."

"You guys played hard," my father said, kindly, and he pulled out onto the road for home.

•   •   •

For all Brian Barnes's worldly experience he apparently hadn't seen what doctoring in a small American town was all about. It was the jokesters and hangers-on and volunteers my brother introduced him to out in the rain, but it was also the frightened vigil of a ten-year-old boy on our front porch, and the nameless face of shock and sorrow that turned a family speechless as a stump. Danny went up the steps and said something to the boy who stood riveted against the rail post. Brian followed Danny inside, springing on the balls of his feet, hungry for the next thing.

It was dusky in the waiting room. The patient straddled one of the metal-framed armchairs. He was literally built like a barrel, and the air gasping in and out of his quivering mouth stung the atmosphere in the room. Post vomit bile. To see someone else in fear is a terrible thing. You lose your bearings for a second, there's nothing to grab onto, nothing to say. You're a bird on one wing.

"Melanie, get me some water," my mother directed calmly, not taking her eyes from the man's face. How she could be that close, holding somebody twice her size across the chair like that was beyond me. He looked like he had a two-by-four rammed down his back. "Right now!" Mom said.

I passed by the drug room on the way down the hall to the sink in the treatment room. Dad was in there holding a vial at eye level, pulling yellow fluid into a syringe through a needle long enough to pass all the way through my thigh, it looked like. I got the water and went back out to the waiting room. Brian hung back in the far corner, his arms folded hard across his chest, his head locked into position as if he'd thrown his neck out of joint.

"Here, Mom." The man was dazed, drooling. "Here, Mom," I repeated, holding the glass of water toward her.

"Drink it, Mel, you'll feel better." I don't know how, but I drank it straight down.

"Good girl," she said, "now, come over here, we're going to need your help."

My father came out and gently lifted the man's eyelids one after the other. His eyes were murky as a sick dog's.

"Let's try it, Marj," he said, softly. Then he gave me that commanding look that I conjure up to help me only when I'm on the edge and need to pull myself together. "Don't let him fall, Mel." The needle disappeared into the man's ragged chest. I remember seeing my father's arm drive down and Mom riding the beefy mass out of the murk and into the clear. The room could have been packed with everybody in town, and I wouldn't have noticed one of them.

"There," my father breathed easily, "I think we're in business." A hushed cry went up from the corner under the coat rack behind the door. A woman, scrawny as a grackle, huddled against the wall. She sniffled in noisy spasms and crept up behind us as if she were about to peer over the edge of the Letchworth Gorge. "Harp," she chirped, and fell to her knees, hugging the man's legs. He sat up and held his own in the chair as my mother pulled me back to give the couple room, while Dad checked him with the stethoscope.

"You could have died," the wife whimpered, "you could have died."

"Shut up, and stop sniveling," he growled without looking at her, his eyes staring out on the gray day through the distant windows in the reception nook. My mother winced and squeezed my hand. "I'm walkin' outa here, Doc, now," he said, and lifted himself out of the chair with a rumbling cough. His wife scrambled to her feet.

"But Harp!"

"Shut up, I said. Where's Bobby?"

She raised one hand to her mouth and motioned toward the door with the other. He must have spotted his son through the front door glass, because he relaxed for a moment and said, 'okay' before turning to my father.

"What do I owe ya, Doc?"

"Just a call when you get home. I want to see how you are in an hour. Then I want you to see Doctor Berundi for a complete cardiac exam at St. Jerome in the morning. I'll set it up."

"Don't go to hospitals," he said, and ambled to open the door. He caught his wife by the shoulder as he reached for the knob and glared at her. "Dry up, and don't tell Bobby nothin'. Nothin' happened, understand?" He pulled her outside, and I can still see her scuffed penny loafers barely touching the threshold as she followed him out to the porch. The kid snuck under his mother's arm and the three of them trundled down the walk in the misty rain, bent low as they passed the volunteer firemen and crossed the street to a faded red pickup.

The rescue chief, Dale Stockard, met Dad on the porch out of the rain. They stood, watching the pickup drive off, and shrugged the way men living in small towns together for years do, their needs for words minimal, meaning being rounded into their shoulders over the years.

"Takes all kinds," Stockard said.

"Where'd you find them?"

"Out on the Angling Road, front of Sawyer's place. She'd gone in to call."

"Well, we'll either get sued, or we'll never see 'em again," my father laughed a little. "Time to get back to the table and see if there's some coffee left, at least. Want to come in?"

"Naw, me'n the boys got to get the vehicles back. Costs a damn mint to take 'em out."

"Good work, Dale." My father waved to the volunteers, still standing in a gaggle under the dripping evergreens.

"See ya, Doc."

"Not again today, I hope."

"Say, that Brian Barnes with your Danny?"

"Yeah, you know Brian?" Dad broke into a puzzled grin.

"Saw him on the TV, if that's the fella, maybe last week."

"What was he doing on TV?"

"Talkin' about something, I guess, but I'm sure now it's him."

"Huh," Dad laughed. "Well, he's still talking, Dale, and we haven't had the TV on all day!"

We resumed what was left of dinner, but we couldn't locate Brian right away; I guessed he'd gone for a walk. It would have suited him, a walk in the rain. Instead, he was upstairs in the bathroom where he said he'd barfed his brains out. When he came down, we all pretended we didn't notice he'd been gone. The double chocolate cake was already sliced into large wedges, and mother brought in a fresh pot of perked coffee and a half-gallon box of Sealtest vanilla fudge ice cream. Brian flopped down in his chair and let the wind trail out of himself in a long slow melody like he didn't intend to breathe in again for a very long time. My mother poured the first steaming cup for him and set it close so the steam actually rose into his face. He nodded gratefully, and we waited for him to speak. He looked so self-absorbed that I was tempted to lean over and pinch the hint of his double chin, but I was afraid he'd bang his elbow on the table or knock something over. In spite of myself, I felt warm and cuddly toward him.

"I can't believe it," he finally sighed. "You saved that man's life." He sighed, shallower, picking up a little steam. "Never saw it close like that, the eye of the dying man rolling in on itself like a slimy marble."

"No wonder you tossed your cookies, Brian!" Mom blurted it right out there, and we started laughing so hard we were crying, Brian too.

•   •   •

I saw Brian Barnes on my own two summers later at the Silver Bay Aesthetics Workshop on Lake George. I wrote to ask a special favor, a reference, since I believed he could help me overcome my lack of experience. For whatever reason, he did it, and I got to spend six days and nights in Intensive Creativity on gorgeous and historic Lake George, for the modest tuition of $629, room and board included. Brian led a workshop on the roots of dramatic discovery in fiction. He encouraged us to throw ourselves into real life, to engage its dramas. He talked about going to Belfast. He talked about living with a rebel cadre in the mountains of Guatemala. *Immersion in real place and time.*

I slept with him on the third night. Truthfully, I thought it might not mean too much, but he was wonderfully considerate and gentle about it, not at all like the way he ate or railed about the writing craft of instinct and grit. His hands felt like Naugahyde smoothing my skin, and he didn't come for nearly an hour, which drove me crazy, even though I'm a very big non-screamer. I laughed hysterically when he said in all sincerity that he felt the earth move. We had the 'ultimate post-modern romance' such as it was possible in a 'cynical world suspended beyond even the salvation of nuclear doom' as he was fond of saying. We saw each other through Brian's residencies at places like Wichita State and Naropa and my college vacation visits to 20 West Main.

Brian published a book of stories titled LIFESAVING BEGINS WITH A STEADY HAND, based on medical practice in a small town. He dedicated it to "The Wells Family, Poets All," but the book lacked a certain insight to the mundane mystery of volunteers standing in the rain, the doctor stabbing a heart on Sunday, the brute-loving wife. My mother had Brian cased that first week-end. His throwing up in the seclusion of the upstairs bathroom, while she gagged on the fumes of a desperate patient, wasn't her idea of a substantial man. I remember how she laughed when Brian reintroduced himself downstairs, like she'd been freed of a burden, but her seeing him as a blowhard hadn't dampened my attraction to him.

•   •   •

My father is retired now, except for the tendrils he holds onto from his forty-six year practice for balance, some hospital consulting, a day a week volunteer stint at the village clinic. I see him in my mind's eye tilted back a bit on his leather LA-Z-BOY, the 35-inch Toshiba my mother bought him for their anniversary fired up with the full spectrum of live color from Yankee Stadium, or Comiskey Park, or Wrigley Field. A base runner dashes around third in a wide arc, arms pumping, head thrust back, striding like a gazelle. Dad pops forward in the LA-Z-BOY: "Go-go-go!" A hoarse stage whisper you can hear from the kitchen where my mother fiddles with utensils on the counter while we talk.

"You know, he turns the sound off sometimes and calls the games until he loses his voice."

I can't tell you how she means this. Is it simply an amusing fact, or a worrisome sign of failing health?

"Did Dad talk much with you about life and death, like that time he drove the big man's heart with the needle?"

"Oh, the Brian Barnes weekend! That was some real action. Your father always said he couldn't have done it alone. He could feel a strange power gathered that day, and he relied on it to make the right diagnosis. He really didn't have much time, you know."

"Yes, Brian was impressed, as I recall," I said, offhandedly.

"Very impressed. But he seemed to miss something, guts, I think, if you'll pardon the expression."

"It's okay, Mom."

"For all that bravado, I expected more of him, frankly."

"Dad did too, I guess."

"Oh, no, Ben got a big charge out of him. He didn't expect Brian to be anything he wasn't. He was surprised about *you* and Brian, but he got used to it. So, what's happened to Brian, anyway? He was such a regular around here for a while; we got quite attached to him, you know."

"Oh, he's heavily involved in something new," I look at Mom's feet. She closes a cupboard door and straightens the row of porcelain canisters along the backsplash.

"SAFE!" My father bellows from the family room. "He was safe by three feet!" He's snarling like he's clinging to the backstop behind home plate.

"You never liked baseball, did you, Mel," Mom says.

"Never," I laugh a little, knowing Mom has tolerated it all these years. "But I love that old fan in there."

"Me too," she smiles, and we go in to the game.

FAMILY TRUST

F ROM the kitchen windows over the sink you could watch the winter sun follow the pale dawn in its lethargic ascent of the Saint Francis Church steeple. Shielded by the church's long roofline, the driveway leading to our barn was often cast in deep blue shadow. The row of maples, their dark trunks wrapped in the thick rough bark of middle age, cast their own darker sentinel profiles across the drive and up the walls of 20 West Main. A set of deep wheel tracks cut through the snow to the barn doors. The barn still housed grain bins and a horse stall, and you could imagine a sleigh, harnessed to a fresh stallion, waiting to take the doctor who built 20 West Main in the 1880s out on rounds.

During the hour before Dad's office opened and the passing of the first school buses, Mom set out orange juice, bananas and canned peaches on the stainless steel counter under the wall cupboards. Sliced whole wheat bread and the butter dish were set by the toaster. Fresh-ground coffee popped in the glass bubble atop the percolator. A pitcher of creamy pasturized milk chilled on the top shelf in the Kelvinator.

Dad, our most consistent early riser, liked coffee and pastries for breakfast and often leaned back against the counter as he ate. Barbara Ann, 16, tried to control her weight by refusing to eat before lunch time. Melanie, 11, was unpredictable and might make eggs and bacon with Mom and eat double portions of everything, or appear at the very last minute for a slug of juice and a bite of toast.

Breakfast, I rarely missed, and on that Thursday morning in February the menu included pancakes rippled with blueberries. I stirred milk into the batter, making an easy-to-pour texture. As I ladled the batter onto the pre-heated grill, it flowed out symmetrically and began to whisper and bubble immediately. I wanted the blueberries to warm and expand, but not fry into mushy coins. I flipped three pancakes and crossed to the window just as the silhouette of a man slid sideways through the near barn door, fixed open by ice build-up.

At first I thought it was Dad, since his car was bedded on that side. What I saw didn't look like Dad, however, and his rhythmic feet tapping down the back stairway into the kitchen assured me that Dad couldn't be out in the barn.

"Morning, Dan, how'd you sleep?"

"Hi, Dad, algebra test, seventh period."

"I saw your light on when I turned in. You're due to hit one out of the park. Your mother's got the coffee on, I see."

"It's all yours, Dad. You might need an extra cup for the guy in the barn, too."

"What's that?" He looked at me quizzically and then out the kitchen window at the front of the barn. The sun peeked high enough to shoot a band of light across his view, and he shielded his eyes with his left hand as he raised the coffee cup to his pursed lips with his right. From his expression I thought he thought I was kidding.

"A man in the barn, eh? Maybe it's old man Judd coming

back for his horse," Dad deadpanned.

"He's been gone awhile, hasn't he?"

"'Bout eight years now, but you never know," he said.

"Well, I saw somebody, and he went right into your side, ten minutes ago, maybe." I slid the browned pancakes out of the pan onto my plate and turned off the gas.

Dad sipped the coffee. He was careful not to drip any on his blue and dark-green striped tie. I glanced down at his polished oxblood Nettletons and creased charcoal wool slacks. He was ready for morning office hours. I felt guilty for introducing the day's first complication, but there was someone in the barn, maybe a disoriented patient, or a car thief.

"I'll go see," I said suddenly.

"Barefoot?" Dad jibed. "Put a piece of toast in for me, and I'll be right back. That barn has been haunted since old Judd died and forgot to take his pony with him."

The Judds had kept the old man's favorite Arabian horse in our barn after a fire leveled their barn in '49. Mom fed and curried the mare all through the fall and into the early winter when Judd got the new barn raised. After all the pampering, the horse refused to return across the street with Judd the first time he came after her. She kicked and nipped at him the second time, and my mother finally led her calmly home and promised to visit often to keep the horse happy. She also bargained with Judd for riding time, and her relationship with the Arabian mare outlasted Judd's. In fact, Judd never quite forgave Mom for stealing the heart of his favorite horse, and every so often he would turn up in our barn acting irritated and confused. Dad joked that it wasn't Judd, but his ghost.

"He's a lot bigger than Judd," I warned, as Dad headed out the back door. "Want me to come too?"

"Don't forget the toast, Danny," he said without looking back as he closed the door.

•   •   •

Tension sparks darker elements of the imagination. Your mind reassembles floating scenarios to explain the unknown. An ill patient wanders into the barn to lie down and die. A vagabond goes in to sleep in the car, or steal it. A distraught husband lurks in the tool room honing his vengeance over the death of his misdiagnosed wife. Et cetera.

Mom, Barbara Ann and Melanie trouped down from the upstairs bathrooms, the girls ready for school, Mom in her robe, hair and make-up done.

"You're not dressed," Barbara Ann announced. The intimation that I'd be late for school rang in her voice. Melanie was too busy sorting through her book bag to notice whether I was clothed or not.

"Yes, he's certainly pushing the clock," Mom joined in, "but Mister Clausen would go into shock to see Danny on time. Where's your father? I thought we might squeeze in a little family time for breakfast."

"Fat chance, Mom." Barbara Ann rushed around the kitchen, picking up her homework from the desk under the Dutch windows. "I'll take a banana, just for you, Mom."

"You need more than that, Hon."

Melanie was slow to awaken fully, and even after half an hour in the bathroom she could maintain a sleepy disinterest to the world around her.

"Where's Dad?"

"Oh, Mel, you're with us!" Mom greeted her. "Your brother is getting ready to reveal his whereabouts, aren't you, Dan."

"He's in the barn," I said.

"And?" Mother quizzed.

"He's been out there for several whole minutes."

"And?"

"Some guy's out there, too."

"What guy, what's he look like?" Barbara Ann stopped flitting around the kitchen and lasered her wide eyes at me. "A convict's loose from the Erie Pen, I heard on WKBW! What's he look like? Green jacket? Shaved head?"

"No, no, I don't think so," I said, seriously unsure about description. Mom didn't like my answer, and deep creases shot through her forehead and into the double lines between her brows.

"It's the ghost of Thomas Judd," Melanie intoned in a Boris Karloff-like voice.

"It's not funny, Mel," Mom scowled. She went to the porch door and peered out the window. "Don't see him, don't see anybody," she said with a kind of hopeful confidence. She turned toward me, and I could tell by the searching look in her eyes that she was about to decide which one of us should call the town cop and who would venture out to the barn.

"Going on fifteen minutes," Mel narrated in a hoarse whisper.

"Stop it, Mel. I don't know how you can be so cavalier at a moment like this," Mom said.

"Got it from Dad," she whispered, hoarsely.

Barbara Ann and I encouraged our younger sister with our laughter.

"You're all insensitive! Your father's in danger, and it's a joke to you. I'm glad he's not here to see it."

"Okay, Mom, now let's not jump to the ghoulish conclusions. We can bet Dad's under control, as usual," I hoped.

"We have to do something," she said. "You're without shoes, Barbara Ann's wearing patent leather today for some reason, and Melanie's playing 'Whispering Streets.' Who's left to be the detective?!" And with that she opened the door and went not too quietly across the porch, down the two steps and over the packed snow path to the driveway. We rushed to the windows to watch Mom boldly disappear into the barn.

"I should have known." Mom returned, slamming the kitchen door. Gone were the worry lines, the teary-eyed determination. "It never pays to let relatives take advantage, there's no end to the need or the trouble."

We Wells children gaped at each other, and Barbara Ann quipped without thinking, "Okay, Mom, you're off my Christmas card list!"

"I'm not a relative, I'm your mother," Mom retorted, and went to the cupboard to take down plates and coffee mugs.

"Okay, sorry, I gotta go." Barbara Ann passed in and out of the laundry room where we hung the coats. She gathered her things and pulled on her padded wool coat.

"Me too," Melanie said cautiously, watching Mom set the oval kitchen table for breakfast. "I've got study hall for geography. Today's Wednesday?"

"Thursday," Mom sighed, moving from counter to table and over to the stove. "Thursday, today's Thursday. Thursday's child knows not the days of the week. Monday's child eats not breakfast. What's Friday's child not do, Dan?"

"Worry," I said. "So, what's up outside?"

"I'm packing up, you guys, if anyone cares." Melanie went to the stove and wrapped her arm around Mom's waist. Mom kissed her good-bye and looked up at the KitKat clock where its black tail swung the minutes away above the archway to the dining room.

"Tomorrow we'll have breakfast together," Mom said.

"Do I have to guess?" I wanted information.

"He's in the car with Cousin Benjy."

"Dad's childhood double?"

"One and the same. Why your grandmother's brother

couldn't come up with his own name for his first son is beyond me, and Cousin Benjy looks and acts just like Ben's grandfather used to, slow." Cousin Benjy had trouble holding jobs, and he traipsed from hospital to hospital, state to state seeking employment as a male nurse. My grandmother said he was a fine nurse and that only his unstable health kept him from being a physician. I never heard anyone else, notably Dad, actually agree with her.

"He afraid to come into the house?"

"We should count our blessings, but it's unnerving, what with the way things are getting these days. I wish your father could be more careful."

"He's got a guardian angel, Mom. Not to worry. Here he comes now."

When Dad opened the door and stepped up into the kitchen, we turned to face him, and in spite of some unspoken sympathy for his situation, we let loose.

"Is it the wacky one, Dad?"

"What did he want, Dad?"

"Did you give him money?"

"What normal person would sneak into your own car and wait for you to come out?"

A look, part blush, part guilt, part irony came over Dad's face. He looked at Mom, his mouth opening for what we were sure was the explanation of the decade.

"I could really use a hot coffee, Marj."

We sagged for a second or two, then quickly resumed our separate senses of direction. Mom turned to get the coffee, Barbara Ann actually accomplished her departure for school, Melanie procrastinated. Mom handed Dad a full mug of hot coffee, black, the way he liked it. "Why don't you sit down, Ben?"

"Got an office full already," he said, impassionately.

"How's Benjy?"

"He's cold, broke, half-sick. Otherwise, tip-top."

She nodded while giving me the 'what's new' look. "And, what else?" She leaned against the stove, arms crossed, a smile teasing the corners of her mouth.

"Well, Ol' Benjy hitched an early ride over from Medina on a tanker. I doubt he's got a way back. I was hoping someone here could drive him home before school." He sipped steadily at the coffee and glanced at the morning paper that lay on the table.

"You're kidding," Mom said. "Dan's late, as it is."

"I'll call Charlie Clausen. Danny's not scheduled for much this morning, are you, Danny?"

He was right, and even though I would have loved an excuse to miss school, Benjy wasn't on the list.

"Good," Dad said, "you need the driving practice, and traffic will be light across Allegheny Road. Might do you some good to spend a little time with Benjy, too. He's down on his luck, for now."

"How much is he down this time, Ben?" Mother unplugged the percolator and poured Dad a refill at the table.

"Farther than we'd want to be. Haven't we got a donut around here? It's going to be a day till lunch."

Mom went to the bread box under the cupboard and lifted out a waxed paper bag. She squeezed it a couple of times without looking inside and set it next to his bare plate. "That's not the point, you know," she said.

"In his case, there may not be much of a point. Danny, let's get moving. You won't miss much school at all, if you get moving. You don't want to leave Benjy out in the barn, do you?"

"Has he showered, lately?"

"Hmm." Dad crinkled a smile while reading the front

page. "Right here," he said, "a man was found frozen to death behind his cow barn over in Wyoming County."

"Okay," I said, "keys in the car?"

•   •   •

Benjy lived on the second floor of a drab three-story Victorian converted to apartments. The staircase was walled in, and getting to the northwest corner to his place required a nearly blind trek up the battered risers and a cautious walk along a crookedly framed hallway to the alcove of his doorway. Inside, it smelled like fried onions. Benjy had dozed the 16 miles to Medina, and after the short walk from the parked car in the cold morning air and the climb up the stairs, he was winded but alert.

"Have a seat," he said. "Clear that chair there. Like some tea?"

I didn't drink tea, but I wasn't going to make him feel inhospitable. He shuffled over to a dresser angled out from the wall to make a counter for the hot plate. While he puttered around, I took in the water-stained ceiling, the yellowed wallpaper, the frosted side window.

Benjy collected things. Matchbooks, cat's-eye marbles, cigar boxes, baseball cards, green juice glasses, cast-iron toys, leather-covered books, thimbles. He wrapped the matchbooks with wide rubber bands. He stacked the cigar boxes on the tops of old oak dressers pushed against the walls. Inside the boxes he kept the baseball cards wrapped in cellophane. Flanking the door, two chrome-plated clothes racks held a platoon of navy-blue pea jackets on wooden hangers. Piles of books, newspapers, movie magazines and hunt club newsletters collected dust under the dressers. In the corner near the frosty window a woolen Army blanket covered a low iron bed frame. I spied the spine of the Rochester phone book under the lumpy pillow.

Benjy had suffered from seizures since adolescence. He had spells and visions that disoriented him unless he maintained his medications. And sometimes even they weren't effective. Prescription-wrapped bottles lined the window sill. I wondered how often he woke in the cold slash of the street light to reach for them.

"Like somethin' in your tea?" Benjy hummed words from the back of his throat.

"What have you got?" I asked, politely.

"Honey it is." He stepped around a pile of laundry and handed me the opaque green cup, tepid to the touch. "Thanks," I said, "tea is different for me."

"Me too," he said. "I like the stronger stuff, but it's early. Haven't been to the garage yet, or the newsstand. Library opens at noon today." He wheezed and snuffed, short of breath.

"So, Medina is a pretty hopping town, I guess."

"Oh," he paused, pulling his hand down around his jowls a couple of times. "I miss the city."

"Really," I said. Benjy was known to talk in parables and riddles, so I didn't feel guilty asking him if there was a particular city.

"Rochester, you know, that was the place, job, nice places to eat, ladies. Your father went to college nearby, before the war, before my travelin' days. More tea?"

Benjy's shoe size was at least 14 triple E. He walked with such light, careful steps that it was hard to imagine him jumping freight trains from a cinder-strewn rail bed or kicking in the locked door of a prostitute with them. He took my empty cup from the arm of the sprung easy chair and walked the few feet to the galley sink, where he put the cup. The bathroom was down the hall, so he kept a full shelf of toiletries above the small fridge wedged into the far corner where the bay window angled back into the wall of the house. He reached for a large canister of talcum powder and came back to sit on the bed near me.

"You collect a lotta stuff," I said.

"Oh my, yes. I wonder if you'd help me sort it sometime. Could be worth somethin'."

"Sure," I said, "just let me know, we can set it up."

"Well," he looked at his assorted possessions and seemed to reconsider his proposal. "Okay," he said, finally. Benjy bent down and untied one shoe with his puffy white fingers, then the other. He slipped one off, held it up and tamped the talc can over the heel, then he tilted it toe-down in his hand and massaged the worn leather body, jiggling the shoe until the whole inside was layered with the powder. He took great pains to do it right. He repeated the process with the other shoe. When he finished, Benjy set them neatly on the floor, toes out, under the bed. He wheezed deeply and swung his dusty white stockinged feet onto the bed as he rolled onto his side.

"You die from the feet up," he said, and closed his eyes.

I waited for something more, and I thought for a minute that I might say something. Then, I stood clumsily, my left foot numb and tingling. So this was how Benjy said good-bye. I pulled the door closed on my way out, lifting on the knob to compensate for the loose hinges. The sour smell of the hallway carpeting drove me quickly down the stairs and out into the winter air.

•   •   •

I started the engine and thought of Benjy rolled up on his narrow cot, nowhere to go, nothing to keep track of but junk. He seemed so different from Dad. Tentative, as if each word and movement were eked out, worried over. You'd never get the story about his ex-wife or his nurse's training. If you were Benjy, you viewed the world through the lenses of a frightened imagination. Inside his head, the good memories were carved into the skull so pain and confusion couldn't misplace them. You protected your possessions against the unpredictable thrashings of your own body. Sparingly, you tended your flimsy tethers to the world, for even the solitary life requires regimens of human contact. I saw Benjy's physical resemblance to Dad, the broad shoulders and chest, the reflections of their family's inherent kindness in their eyes, and in spite of my impulse to avoid a return visit, I knew I would drive back to Medina to sort through things with Cousin Benjy.

I would drive out alone and look for Benjy on his morning rounds of the neighborhood. I would find him sitting behind the greasy window of the one-bay garage where he kept an eye on the lone red gas pump that he operated for customers for a few bucks. I would spot him through the window before he recognized me, have the last chance to turn away. Then, his wide, fleshy face would open and his mouth would hesitate around my name. He would rise, turn the chair cushion over and amble across the street with me to his room, where we would meander in conversation about used cars he'd bartered, or hospital towns in Ohio. I would try to imagine the flashing and screeching of a coming spell he said he could sense like smelling rain in the wind.

On the road near Basom I needed the headlights to get through a heavy squall. In the lights' blinding dance I sensed the shapeless details that dog a man's life. When I got home I said it wasn't so bad, the day with Benjy. There was something gratifying about spending time with a family enigma, but I couldn't explain that.

A couple of years later, Benjy was evicted from his digs in Medina. I was at college, and after New Year's, Dad called to tell me they had found Benjy in the Erie Barge Canal. He had wandered away from the nursing home where Dad had arranged lodging and treatment for him. Night. A blanketing snow. Benjy had stopped taking his medicine.

Six weeks after the small funeral, crisp fifty-dollar bills wrapped in cellophane began to arrive in plain envelopes addressed to Dr. Benjamin Wells. Benjy was true to his namesake even in death. I wondered how conscious he had been about saving up for the solitary generosity we will always remember him by. The fifties arrived sporadically over the years, and Dad passed them on in kind to his three children. He called them dividends from The Wells Family Trust.

MIDDLE GROUND

H ALF way up the creek, my cousin Randy stopped. I was covering his flank in case he flushed a deer and couldn't get a shot. When I came up behind him, he stood, feet spread, shoulders rigid, rifle hanging in his right hand, not turning at the sound of my voice.

"What's up, Rand?"

"I see something weird."

"A track?"

"A foot, I think."

"Naw."

"There!" Randy said, "A woman's foot."

I stared at the receding bank where it rolled under sumac and rose steadily into thickets of brambles and ferns and close-growing trees. I tried to imagine a foot sticking up like a key star in a constellation. "I don't see anything," I said.

"Go up and take a look."

"You go, you saw it, I don't," and then I did see. The foot stuck out, a small demanding signal in an open-toed black shoe. "You asshole," I said, "It's a mannequin. Go look for

69

yourself, and I'll shoot her if she jumps you."

"You're a gas, Col. It's for real, and I'm scared shitless if you want to know."

"All right, relax." I leaned my rifle against the shale ledge and climbed up through the low brambles on the soft, muddy bank between the ledge and the first big pines. The foot protruded from the leaves and humus near the bottom of the gorge. "Yeah, it's a shoe okay, with a foot in it," I called, "want me to pull 'er out for you?"

Randy turned toward the cold, shallow creek. I wanted him to come up beside me, as the outline of the body took shape in a five-foot long mound starting at the exposed foot and running down-stream into the bank. Near my feet, a faded purple veil clung to the yellow and brown leaves. I looked carefully and found an ear half uncovered and a swath of matted hair the same color as the ground. The head, half buried, turned face forward into the bank.

My eyes watered. I wiped them with the back of my hand and motioned for Randy. He froze. I bent down on my left knee and began to pick leaves and mud off the head until her shin was exposed, until I knew the skin was skin, a head with a body attached, something that had happened. A woman alone in the woods in dress shoes, a Sunday hat, a pearl earring, mouth full of dirt.

I got enough of her uncovered to figure she'd been there since early fall. Her dress was torn along her upturned shoulder. A light tan rain coat had been thrown over her. The left side of her head and temple looked dented, the skin ashen and matted with hair. A vision of her crossed my mind: trim in her new outfit, walking on a warm, glistening afternoon, falling from the ledge, or turning an ankle in a chuck hole, or... a man with a rock in his hand, a black bird flashing from thorn bushes, her face turning to catch the fluttering wings, the rock crushing the light.

"Collyn?" Randy's touch shocked me right out of my skin. "Now, what?"

I stood slowly and faced him. I hadn't thought about what to do. In Randy's eyes the flash of fear asked me again. "You don't know her, do you?"

In the split second before I said no, the sounds of my mother's name, my sister's name, my wife's name ran through me. "I'll stay here while you go downstream to the first set of falls," I said. "Cut up that old cow path along the bank to Brandreth's silos, get over to the house and call Dad. He'll know what to do."

I walked down to the water with Randy and then watched him cross and weave his way down the rocky bank to the bend where his red-shirted back disappeared. I spotted a stone on the bottom of a kidney shaped pool upstream from where I stood. The stone would fit in my hand, work as a corn grinder, or a bludgeon. The woman's body behind me was no more than the stone at the bottom of the pool, yet she would reach out from her consequence and move the coroner, the sheriff, the undertaker, a myriad of people connected with her body, her crushed skull, and who knows, maybe make more happen dead than she did alive. Someone would have to know why she was where she was and how she got there.

I tried to recall each step, each sight leading to our discovery of the body, to the uncovering of her head, to feel the woods that stood around me now, knowing the story, already reconciled to the body's interminable life in the ground. I began to feel a part of the bank, the trees, the brown bare stalks of brush, the rocky creek running for no other reason but gravity down the old sloping gorge it had been crafting since rain and snow and spring water ran off in the same direction, before anyone was around to notice. I sat cross-legged on the ground and waited.

Finally, they came around the bend and picked their way up the other side of the creek. Randy, Dad and the Sheriff crossed a short rock bridge and circled me for a moment to look around at the woods and talk. Dad spoke first.

"No deer today, eh?"

"Up there," I pointed.

"See anything on your way in or while you been waiting for us?" Sheriff Wagner was already climbing toward the body. Dad followed him. When they reached the body, they knelt beside it for several minutes and then came back down.

"Can't do much with her here," Dad said. "Better get somebody over here to carry her out. I'll order an autopsy and we can proceed from there." Wagner nodded and pulled a walkie-talkie from his belt. Static cracked the woods.

Dad stood looking into the middle distance between the creek and the woods on the other side. "What the hell do you suppose a middle-aged woman was doing out here in her high heels? Got the feeling she didn't walk all the way. Been here awhile, too. Damned nice place to die, if you have a chance to choose."

"Yeah, but you think she was killed, don't you?"

"Looks like it. Head's been hit with some sort of blunt instrument. You ready to go?"

●   ●   ●

I didn't make it home until after dark. I'd phoned Sally to tell her what happened and that I was eating supper with my folks. She said she had spent a crazy afternoon delivering our dog's seven puppies. Sally had gotten sick to her stomach cleaning up the mess and was glad she could skip supper. I closed the kitchen door behind me and found myself staring at Sally who stood ram-rod straight in the middle of the room. She had washed her hair, and it fell like a sun shower onto her shoulders. Her face was the color of chalk.

"Long day, huh? You all right?"

"Sure, why?"

"Well, you look a little pasty around the gills."

"That's sweet of you, Collyn. So, how was it?"

"You should have seen her, Sal."

"No, I shouldn't have *seen* her, or a dead deer, or any of those car wrecks your father takes you to. I'm not into *morbid*, you know?"

"Who is? I didn't go hunting for a body. The whole thing just happened."

"If your father called and said there was a body in the woods, you would bolt right out there to see. Besides, you were out to kill deer."

"Is there anything I do that you like?"

Her mouth froze. For an instant her eyes flashed a naked awareness of something she saw in mine, something she heard in my voice. Her shoulders slumped. I crossed the floor between us and put my arms around her. She pushed her hands flat against my chest.

"You smell like strawberry."

"You smell like an animal. I've got to check on the new members of the family and go to bed. I'm bushed."

Sally slipped away to her dogs. I stripped my hunting jacket and two layers of cotton and wool shirts and tossed them onto the counter. When Sal came back through from the cellar on her way upstairs, she signaled me to hang up my clothes. Standing in the center of the kitchen, surrounded by the wall cupboards I had built, I checked the time on the antique wall clock we had saved for, searched for, debated over and finally bought as if our lives depended on it. I pulled my thermal shirt over my head and threw it in the corner by the back door. I did the same with my boots, knee socks, pants and boxer shorts. Then I walked the length of my house, turning off lights room by room, and climbed the stairs in the dark. Our bedroom was dark, cool, and I began to shiver as I slid in to bed and snuggled up to Sal. She lay still, and I ran my hand down her narrow torso, her belly as smooth as a lamb's hide stretched over her pelvic bones.

"Please go to sleep, Collyn." She buried her head into her deep pillow.

I wanted to punch her for making my name sound like a reprimand. I rolled onto my back and wrenched the quilt up in my fists. I wanted to cast it off like an old skin and crawl from beneath its cloying warmth and do something. Go out into the cold wet night and listen to the ground squish under my feet, jack deer, fuck somebody's wife.

•　　　　　•　　　　　•

The Night we told Sally's father of our engagement, he sat in his beat up rocker, stocking feet propped on the Kalamazoo wood stove that heated the downstairs.

"What's my little girl goin' to do with a doctor's boy? We all think the world of you, Collyn, but you been trampin' around a while, and that does things to a man. Maybe not right away, but eventually, your feet'll be getting' itchy."

I could take anything Sally Fitzsimmon's father said in stride, but she sat stone still at the table not taking her eyes from my face while her father's methodical tone and rhythm made whatever he said seem more like gospel than a father's cautionary drivel. After an hour of "heart to heart," as Fitz liked to call it, the big man squared his feet on the floor, stood and pulled me into a hard handshake and slapped me on the back so hard my face crashed into his chest. Hot tears rushed across my eyes.

On the way back to town I aimed my MG down the country roads behind the high beam of one headlight. At the time I had wanted to follow it out of the county, west past Lake Erie and into the pulp of America. I swore I could feel the bottoms of my feet itch down in the cowling of the rattling convertible.

When Fitz rolled his John Deere down a steep embankment he had negotiated without incident for twenty-four years and crushed his chest, Sally wouldn't talk about it or refer to him in anything but the present tense. "He'll always be alive, no matter what, and he'll always love me and me him." Somehow Fitz's death lived in our house, in me, that was the way it felt. Sally treated me with a new deference. It seemed as if Fitz had rolled part of me under with the tractor, as if Sally in all her talk against death were courting it, going toward the image of her father that grew in purity and perfection at my expense, as if I were fading to a hollow likeness of Fitz. Only in her dreams could she sleep with Fitz and as she denied during the day having had him at night, she denied me, too, not wanting to confuse her loyalties.

Sally's breathing flowed evenly, the pause between breaths a long beat of silence in my ears. I didn't know what death felt like, but if it could stuff you full of leaves and mud and stop the senseless scream you felt coming from nowhere it might be better than sleep.

• • •

One evening in early December, I asked Sally what she wanted for Christmas.

"I want you to do something with your life, Col. Do what

you want to do."

"That's a funny present."

"No, not really."

"But I thought I was doing it."

"If you can't fool me, why try to fool yourself? Teaching bores you. You're too old for baseball and too lazy for medicine. It makes you restless, frustrated, and you make me that way, too. It's no good."

"Everything doesn't get worked out at once, you know."

"Who's talking about miracles? You have to start somewhere. Think about it. Give yourself something for me, and I'll love you for it. Maybe you can save our marriage."

"I could bring Fitz back. Would that do?"

Sally rushed at me from the caned rocker. Her eyes tore through me like a twenty-two shell, her flailing hands just missed my face, and I grabbed her wrists. We leaned into each other, face to face. "You don't have to cut me to pieces, I'm not bloody meat! I'm your wife, you bastard!" She broke free, shaking like a wet dog. I went out to the barn.

•   •   •

Randy and I got two deer before the season ended. We gutted and cleaned them in my barn. Several kids from the high school dropped by to see the carcasses hanging upside down. They didn't stick around for the butchering.

Randy asked if the cops had identified the woman, if anyone had claimed the body or come forward with information. I had managed to keep the body and the case off my mind for awhile. Suddenly, I was angry that he had reminded me.

"Doesn't Uncle Bob have any clues or ideas?"

"He's a doctor, not a detective."

"Well, come to think about it, it's the same difference in a way, diagnostician, detective."

I looked up at Randy from the whetstone where I was sharpening the blade of my six-inch, bone-handled knife.

"So, Col, what are you getting Sally for Christmas? A real surprise, I bet."

"Yeah, I'm thinking about putting a bullet between my eyes for her." I stood and wheeled the knife at the barn wall. It hit point first but at an angle and it fell to the floor. Randy hesitated before retrieving the knife for me. We made fast work of the deer and had them laid away in the storage freezer before the afternoon made its sunless retreat. I asked Randy to stay for supper, but he wanted to get home early to clean up for a party in Rochester. As he got into his Fairlane, I leaned on the fender and asked if he'd like to see the northwest, go to Vancouver.

"You and Sal taking a trip?"

"Not exactly, I just wondered if you had an interest in taking off."

"Oh, yes and no. I mean, we're into the Christmas season, and the store's really humming. I've got management responsibilities now, you know."

"Yeah, I know." I backed away from the car. Randy tried to rekindle the small talk, but I waved him off and went to close the barn doors. I listened to his engine start and the crunch of tires on gravel as he backed down the driveway. The barn smelled of clean, fresh meat. We did the gutting well, not puncturing the digestive tract or making a mess of the organs. I'd known Randy since we were kids. At times I felt like his brother. We went to the same high school, played football together. Once, we shared a girl friend. I drew the rough plank doors together on their oiled overhead track and rollers, dropped the six inch bolt through the latch and turned toward the low back side of the house, its square blank windows waiting for me to put the lights on. Randy could go screw himself.

I anticipated pan frying fresh venison fillets with peppers, onions and diced garlic, but as I entered the kitchen the odor of simmering beef-vegetable soup and baking corn bread changed my plans. Sally had vowed that she wouldn't cook or eat deer meat in her house, but she made no prohibition against me doing it, so it looked like whoever got the kitchen first could fix and eat whatever he or she wanted.

•   •   •

"Vancouver? Why Vancouver?" she asked over a steaming table spoon of broth.

"Never been there, and I like the sound of Van-*coooo*-ver."

"There are lots of far away places you've never been with nice sounding names."

"Name two."

"Singapore. Rio de Janeiro."

"Christ, that's lots of time and money and who knows what else besides you liking the names. I couldn't fucking drive to either one."

"Oh, Col." She started up from the table.

"Please Sal, sit down, I'm sorry, I didn't mean it like that."

She settled back and opened her face to me. "Yes, you did, Collyn, but it's all right. You should say things the way you mean them even if it hurts me."

"You mean that?"

"Can't you see?"

We softened on the shrill edge of her voice. In our earnest talk until midnight we promised to be more sensitive with each other. The vows worked through a holiday season that put us into the heart of a bitter, snowy winter. A storm closed school and Sally got caught at her mother's for two days. I opened the ATLAS OF NORTH AMERICA and traced routes, historic land markers and the network of state parks all across the northern United States. I circled the place names with a magic marker. Fargo, Council Bluffs, Cheyenne, Coeur d'Alene. There was a park in the Black Hills where I imagined camping under a high, brittle sky, the night pierced by the cries of Crazy Horse's ghost and the drumming hoof beats of one hundred-year-old buffalo.

My first sight of Vancouver would be exhilarating, but I couldn't decide how to come upon it from the best vantage point. From Coeur d'Alene, I could cut north along re-lined secondary roads to Canada and head west through a series of north and south running valleys, or shoot directly west on super highways. By late evening I had a mileage chart and rough daily budget sketched on graph paper. Something about the Lewis and Clark Expedition was surfacing in my mind when the fuzzy silent lights of Sally's VW brushed the side windows. I watched the light disappear and waited. She pounded up onto the drifted-in porch. I listened to her swear at the frozen storm door before I got up to kick it free of its icy frame.

"Collyn, you haven't shoveled an ounce of snow."

"Welcome home, dear. I've been so busy counting snow flakes and feeding puppy dogs that I haven't had a chance to locate the snow shovel. Got the driveway plowed though."

"So, get out of the doorway and let me in, I'm freezing. The heater broke. I had to scrape ice from the inside of the windshield with my comb for god-sakes. My feet are absolutely numb."

"The heater's not broken, Sal, Veedubs don't have heaters."

She had to check the dog and her brood in the cellar and put on a tea kettle before sitting down in a cold heap at the dining room table. "What's all of this, a geography assignment?" She let her knee-length parka fall over the back of her chair.

"Charting courses for Vancouver."

"Vancouver, again, in the middle of this weather. Honolulu, Bermuda, Miami Beach even, anything but snow, cold, this north."

"I'm not going tonight."

"Why go anytime?"

I looked at the red and blue lines intersecting and crawling like veins and arteries across the map. "I thought we'd worked this out, about doing something I wanted to do, for me and for you. Remember?"

"Collyn, I'm so tired. How could you think about leaving me, running away on your selfish search now? What if I needed you and you were on the road some place, who knows where? I almost ran into the ditch a hundred times just trying to get home in this crazy storm, and you're on a fantasy trip."

"I'll put this stuff away. How about a cup of hot tea with lemon and honey?"

I went into the kitchen and took down the orange pekoe from the cupboard. I wanted to crush the little box in my hand. When I brought the mug of tea out to the table, Sally's head lay across her folded arms. She looked like a rag doll with her hair tousled out over her elbows onto the grained table top. She lifted her head slowly to look at the mug and flopped down again.

"Your mother must have talked you to death."

"No. It was the other way around for once," she muttered. "I never knew she was such a good listener and she's all alone, too, but it doesn't seem to bother her." Sally encircled the mug with her hands and sat up. "We talked about Daddy. I talked a lot about you. Mother says I have the two of you transposed."

"You've been transposing me? Wow."

"Just sit down and listen for a change." Sally's slow gray eyes hung their full weight on me. I sat facing her. "You are confused with each other in my mind or maybe my heart. I don't know really, but it hurts, and I haven't been loving toward you. I have strange dreams about you, but you're always named Fitz and you're older like him, too. And you keep calling me, but I can't reach you. Does that sound crazy? Mother says if things get worse, I should talk with a doctor."

"Worse?"

"You know, *worse*. I lie in bed next to you and I can almost see your mind working over that dead body in the woods, trying to make connections. It makes me feel cold, like sooner or later you're going to think of me as a body, and then I think of Daddy, and I cry way down inside, so you won't hear me, so I won't hear me. Col, don't look that way. I'm just trying to explain, to say what I feel."

I leaned back from the table, leaving my hands face down on its surface. Sally was talking about divorce and dying. I looked into her face. She was talking to the wall behind me, her eyes flicking as if acknowledging the wall's attention.

"Sal, you're exhausted. Let's go to bed. We can talk about all this in the morning over fried eggs and bacon."

"I won't sleep. I'll just lie there."

"I'll make love to you."

"No, you won't. You're going away, remember?"

We sat staring through the soft yellow light cast by the early American chandelier. The table seemed to drift apart from the crack down the center between its main leaves, taking Sally off toward the kitchen, carrying me back into the dark living room. If we crashed through the walls of the house and out into the January snow, we could sail forever on separate ice flows to the other side of the world where we would meet again, back to back.

•   •   •

Inside the snowbound house we moved like careful ghosts, both trying to be quiet, trying not to find ourselves milling around in the same room at the same time. The radio's innocuous chatter filled the downstairs with reports of storm conditions and nostalgic storm stories of yester-year. I imagined the great silence that would stuff the house like cotton when I turned it off, but the voices were replaced by the low, incessant chords of the wind in the lines and the bare trees. Conspiracy sang along the eaves and along the barn walls. I missed my sixteen-year-old history students.

Sally wandered through the living room from the stairway door. I followed her to the kitchen. When she bent into the refrigerator, I eased behind her. She rummaged through half-empty cartons and bottles and fruit jars until she backed out with the milk. I folded my arms under her breasts and nuzzled her loose hanging hair. She started to say something and I felt a rumble of sound, but she sighed instead. I held her tighter. She laid her head back and turned around.

The phone rang as Sal looked into my eyes. She held her gaze. I knew it was my father with the news I'd been waiting for, and I knew that my answering would kill the question in Sal's eyes. The ringing stopped, and she pressed her mouth to mine.

It was cold out where the snow was busy burying all the hearts in the world, the ones I imagined and the ones I could hear beating.

A LANGUAGE OF THE SOUL

THE wind back-handed the Honda toward the center line and Deidre swung back just as it let up. She felt the front tires grip the road surface hard and jerk her toward the shoulder. She squeezed the steering wheel, cranking left, too far. The car zipped across the center line, and if another car had been coming the other way, she'd have crashed head-on. Frightening, the vision of glare, grillwork, head shadows behind a curtain of windshield, so close. The right front tire caught the high, ragged edge of pavement overlapping the narrow shoulder and the steering wheel whacked her palms hard. She'd be darned if she'd go off the side of this stupid road out here, driving home from a party. The back wheel slammed stones into the wheel well. The whole right side caught the dropped edge and she hit the brake pedal, hard, scared, both feet. How fast? How could you screw up a straight road? The speedo's orange glow. The dark form of the deer vaulting the hood, suspended, statuesque, a snap of the leg bone from the glass.

Ken Jacobs, rode out to the scene with the sheriff. He

wore pants over his pajama bottoms. He stood in the dry ditch, cutting the soles of his feet on sharp weeds that slice through his knitted slippers. Sensation crept along his skin first, from foot to forehead, then deep inside his flesh, inside his bones. Feral odor covered his blond Deidre, the bloody hair matted across her face. His voice deserted him as the sheriff guided him to the backseat of the cruiser.

The next day *The News* ran front-page photos of the accident. Ken studied them with intense disbelief. The big doe was lodged halfway inside the Honda where the form of his daughter was barely visible beneath the animal. How could that new car be crumpled like a lunch box?

Ken sat through the meeting with the funeral director, half listening to his wife, Evelyn, make the decisions about the casket, whether of oak veneer or of burnished stainless steel. What would the silky gray lining dappled by pink hearts do for his girl now? She had that new car for graduation; that was his symbol of love for her. The chest of lavender sweaters at the foot of her bed told the story of her blossoming. What about that? Evelyn pinched his forearm and he rose stiffly from the chair and leaned against her.

At the lip of the open grave he noticed details. In his mind he counted the perfect red rosebuds draping the closed coffin. He analyzed the scissor hinge mechanism of the gurney under the coffin, the chartreuse carpet that covered the actual dirt edge of the grave itself making a kind of common-looking entry as if to a cellar. He counted fifteen pairs of open-toed shoes. A pair of legs in black stockings marked by dark red painted nails brought his eyes up into the face of a woman, familiar but nameless, who wept.

Ken watched patterns of light and shadow hopscotch on the ceiling over the bed where he lay propped on three pillows.

Half the leaves had fallen already and the streetlights, blocked all summer by full foliage, streamed through the disrobing tree limbs like wind itself. He thought of reading the shadows like one would read the signs of tea leaves inside the rim of an empty cup.

"Go to sleep, Ken."

"Can't "

"Won't help anything, you know."

"I'm not looking for help."

"You can't change things."

"If I can't sleep, I can't sleep."

"Grief and mourning are so hard, so personal."

"Everything's personal, isn't it."

Before Evelyn cleaned out the room, Deidre's scent lingered in the covers of her bed. Drawings she made in art class were tacked to the wall opposite the double windows where the rising sun brought their streaks of color to life. The lamp still glowed in the alcove of bookshelves, but her school books had been replaced by decorator magazines.

Ken paraded each of Deidre's days through his mind, tried to wrap the feeling of her around him, but as he leaned on the doorframe of her redecorated room his memories of her bled into his own loneliness, and he had to fight the depressive attraction to slouch into her room and lose himself.

Drives to the accident scene calmed his anguish and seemed to give him purpose. It fed the part of him that kept the part of her in him alive. He tethered hickory limbs into a sturdy cross and drove the cross into the edge of lawn above the ditch where Deidre died. Ken meditated at the spot on his way home from work, sometimes getting home late for dinner. He placed a fresh bouquet of wild flowers in a vase and anchored it to the cross with a loop of twine, nothing fancy. As the days shortened and the nights got colder, Ken stayed later, missed dinner often.

Jerry Thrace sat in the darkened alcove of the upstairs bedroom where he and his wife slept during the warmer months until they moved into the cozy room off the kitchen for the winter. Even though he had purchased the 24 acre farm for back taxes and the dream of getting back to his roots, twelve years of sprawl had taught him the shortsightedness of his vision. Now, all he had to do was wait for the next car to sweep its lights across his property to remind him that he couldn't move far enough out into the country. He had to admit he'd been more than tolerant about the cross and the repeated visitations of the dead girl's father, not to mention the reporters and occasional curiosity seekers who came to witness the 'site of the tragedy'. Just last week, a woman calling herself an author rang the bell to ask if she could take some shots of the cross with him and his wife standing in the background, a kind of "suburban gothic," she'd literally beamed at him. He suspected she had already gotten that sad, grieving father lined up for some kind of 'shot', too. The bitch would put it all together in a big Sunday spread, or worse, get them together for an interview on a TV talk show. He could imagine. The night of the wreck had been entirely enough. Jerry wanted it all to end.

"Jerry, come to bed."

"It's well past time to end this charade."

"Let's not get all worked up, again."

"Grief has trespassed on our place long enough."

"Ignore it for a while longer, nothing good can come of whatever you might do."

"Next thing, there'll be a grief cult out there, TV making

us into monsters."

"You know, my mother always said if you expect the worst, it will happen."

Jerry closed the bathroom door and let the warm water soothe his aching hands. He didn't know but that she was right. Ignore the guy. He was suffering on his own clock. The weather's getting cold. Sooner or later there would be a way to get rid of the cross and the guy without making a federal case out of it. Besides, shouldn't the cross be where the body is buried? If we had crosses marking the spots where people actually got killed, we couldn't navigate a mile of highway without running into somebody's grave. Just our family alone would be spread out along the roads of three states. You'd lose track, couldn't visit or set out geraniums. Hell, you'd get killed yourself just trying to keep up with all the markers. Why should we be villains for not wanting our front yard to become a gravesite?

Ken couldn't drive the narrow paths between cemetery lots of gravestones without losing his bearings. Once he found Deidre's gravestone, he was swept by confusion and overcome by the weight of stillness he felt coming from the ground. All those carefully defined plots, ordered like a subterranean Cloverdale, stirred anxiety and anger and smeared whatever picture, whatever gesture he harbored of Deidre. He needed a moment of her, and all of time could change everything else but that. The roadside cross reassured him on each visit, and Ken seemed incapable of projecting into a future absent of the visitation ritual. He felt a spiritual transcendence as he knelt at the cross. The barriers of time and place melted away and he felt something, a language of the soul, take control.

Ken noticed the shadowy movement in his peripheral vision before he stood to face it. The long center shaft of Deidre's cross fit snugly into the grassy hole, and he leaned on it as a tired old man might lean on a cane for support. The shadow stopped several feet up the long slope of ground.

"Name's Jerry Thrace."

"Ken Jacobs."

"Ken, I got to tell you, this cross is going to have to go sometime, soon. I think I know how you feel, but it ain't just you. It's the media types. They think this is some kind of prime time story. Your kid's accident, your grief, my wife and my's role as who knows what? Now, I smoothed out the ruts from the accident, and I chased away any number of curiosity seekers, but I don't think a private property owner has any obligation to tend somebody else's memorial on his own land."

"Mr. Thrace, I appreciate your understanding, deeply."

"And I don't want you out here freezin' to death or somethin'. So, what's the plan?"

"I hate to be so vague, but I don't know. I guess I'm going to kneel down here and listen for awhile."

"Listen?"

"Yeah."

The situation wasn't working out like anything Jerry figured it might. Ken Jacobs wasn't self-righteous; didn't go wacko. The guy acted like there was nothing unusual, like he was standing on common ground. Jerry watched Ken use the cross for balance as he bent carefully to his knees, close his eyes and tilt his head ever so slightly, as if listening to a sound far away. Jerry looked toward the distant woods and looked back at Ken, kneeling, murmuring. Jerry began to feel like an intrusive witness and as he turned toward his house he felt a tremendous emptiness inside.

On the drive home Ken felt the damp spots on his pants knees with the palm of his free hand. A suffocating weight was passing. He took the turn-off to the outer city loop that would take him to the other side of town and the cemetery. His headlight beams illuminated the stone faces of family names, and he counted carefully the rows until he eased the car to a stop at her grave. He shut off the engine, killed the lights. He got out and went to the trunk where he'd laid the cross an hour before. As he lifted it from the dark, the cross felt more like a tangle of limbs than a lightening rod to God, but as he pushed it into the soft earth at the edge of Deidre's stone, Ken felt the divine sensation run through his hands and he knew in his heart that he was doing the right thing, bringing his spiritual longing to this garden of stones where he would be free.

The snows of December filled the shallow ditch and covered the knoll where the cross once cast its shadow in the passing headlights of summer. Jerry missed the cross in a way he couldn't explain. He recalled the night he had gone out to chase the man and the cross from his yard, but as he stood in shin deep snow, looking into the distant ice covered trees, Jerry wondered what it would be like to love a child, to hold her so close, you could make God pay attention to your losing her. He shivered at the penetrating cold and wondered at how his visit to the cross that night had strangely affected him. Hadn't he heard something beyond the man's murmuring? Tonight, he decided to let the wind tear at the icy trees, and to wait longer, listen harder, think of somebody in a way that would inspire him to make a cross and drive it into the ground.

CLOSE TO THE EARTH

T HE helicopter wheeled low out of the sky and whacked a course right over my head on its way over the woods. It wouldn't be enough, turning the old garden turf for planting, without a chopper spying on me. The camera pod stretched out like a black spear under its belly and protruded beyond the nose. As it went over, I looked up and bared my teeth. They could put that shot in the war-on-drugs files.

Anne called from the back deck, but I couldn't hear what she said. She often shouted comments or instructions when I worked outside, and I usually had to guess what she wanted, or pretend I hadn't heard her at all. Now, I knew she was already on her way out.

"They've been over a couple times during the week, and there was that day they circled the woods. I heard them." Anne stood outside the garden fence, an anxious look on her face, the look that twisted or froze whatever it was I was going to say to make her feel better.

"Fuck'm." I wiped my sweaty chin against my shoulder.

"Oh, fine, that'll really help."

"Well, what else, we're helpless down here."

It was an old argument born out of stubbornness and the Lord's will, I'd come to believe. My brother, Barry, had come back from the war with physical wounds that wouldn't heal right and a head that didn't fix.

"I don't know why you insist, Dan. It's dangerous. Stupid!"

"Don't want to hear it."

"We could go to jail."

"Unlikely."

Anne rubbed the back of her leg with the crown of her bare foot as she glared at me before turning abruptly for the house. I bent over the short-handled pitchfork and turned another clump of last year's crust. The garden needed mulch and manure, but my truck hadn't passed inspection and I suddenly had doubts about driving it over to Krebs' farm to load up. Out back, three hundred yards, or so, Barry's marijuana patch needed tending. It would be smart to turn it under and forget about the whole damned business.

"Dad." Now, it was Little Barry peering between his hands where he leaned against the fence.

"Don't bend that fencing in any more than it is already, please." I squinted into his chubby face.

"Dad," he said in the same tone, continuing to lean on the fence. "Were they buzzing us, like Uncle Barry buzzed Vietnam?"

"That's just a National Guard helicopter, nothing to worry about." I sure didn't want to get into Barry's war stories with my ten-year-old, but I recognized my boy's curiosity and sense of connection between the chopper and Barry. I also knew that the buzzed, story-telling Barry was the only one Little Barry remembered. Since I grew up as Barry's younger brother, I had to make major adjustments to deal with the fragments of his life as the disabled veteran. In 1972, he had been reported as missing in action, then killed in action, then AWOL, then wounded and recovering in West Germany. By the time he got home, he had a Technicolor memory and zero ambition. Wearing the tie-dyed T-shirts and cut-off jeans he rarely washed, Barry floated into our lives on a fog bank of dope, the only way he said he could be "motorable." A brother starting a new family, I took him in, no question.

I must have tuned out Little Barry without realizing it. "Dad," he whined, "I'm talking to you."

"Yes, I know. What?"

"I said, are they coming back?"

Bending over the fork again, I turned the dirt along the garden timbers near Little Barry's feet. We were close enough to whisper, and I wondered whether the Guard chopper was only flying over on a weekend training flight. And, I wanted to brush off the worries of a kid overdosed on his uncle's tales of air raids and drug busts.

"I don't know, I hope not, but if they do, maybe it's a sign." I turned the fork over and over, spiking it back into the dirt, hard.

"What sign, Dad?"

"I don't know," I said, knowing exactly what I meant; "a sign is all."

Anne's voice drifted out from the deck; Little Barry pulled away from the fence and ran up toward the house. I jabbed the fork into the ground, but instead of following him, I walked out to the perimeter of the woods and found the overgrown path that paralleled our property line on the south, crossed a seasonal run-off, circled a clump of willows and rose through a stand of white pines before it opened onto an overgrown field where Barry's marijuana patch thrived and continued to grow wild after we institutionalized him. The calm of the place always struck me; it was like an idea coming over you, yet it was real.

Under the overhanging pines, the ground made a gentle hump, and Barry had a way of snugging the small of his back against it so that his legs felt comfortable. With his hands folded behind his head, he could stretch out there for hours, looking up through the pine boughs into the sky. He was so close to the earth he seemed a natural part of it. When the weather was good and I didn't have to work, I sat beside him and tried what Barry called the 'to be' method. Drawing on joints fat as pine cones, we talked about the house we grew up in seven years apart in age. I used to wait for the bathroom as he mimicked the Ipana toothpaste song: 'brusha, brusha, brusha'. He insisted he didn't remember singing the dumb jingle.

We often talked about Dad's accident and the big lawsuit that sapped the life out of him. Barry thought he had gotten careless after too many years at the radiator plant and dumped the acid on himself. "The company's not always in the wrong," he said, "even when they oughta be."

Barry would send dopey smoke skyward and watch it thin out into the air. "Ain't no where to go but up," he'd say. "To be, is just to be, Danny. Trouble with Annie, she wants to make life a picture of something, somewhere else. She should be out here, with us, turning smoke into sky."

I got nervous when he talked about her like she was separate from me, but I felt what he meant a little too clearly. I could feel her drifting up and dissipating. You don't want to see things about your wife that compromise the being you want to believe she is. If she was trying to live a picture, I didn't want to look too close for fear I wouldn't see myself in it.

"There's truth in wine, hope in dope." Barry's wisdom wasn't far from 'brusha, brusha,' but we could laugh together at how ridiculous things were, and I miss that. Barry, with my help, petitioned the courts to use marijuana for medicinal purposes to cope with the pain in his legs, and to quell the visions in his head that made him cry. They didn't want to set a precedent, they said, even though they sympathized and understood, they said. As far as I was concerned, we were proceeding on a course of necessity and mercy. Long after it was clear that Barry needed care beyond the panacea of homegrown weed, the unruly garden of cannabis flourished. How my brother surrendered his youth, his health, and his ideas of living close to the earth were all symbolized in the tenacious plants beyond the white pines. When I stepped into the waist high weeds to untangle a gutty marijuana plant, I felt its roots hold against my hand.

•   •   •

Anne lifted a steaming casserole dish from the oven and set it on the pad in the middle of the table. Salads and half-slices of Italian bread were already on the plates.

"Thought you'd like lasagna after that hard work in the garden. Careful, it's hot."

Daughter Wendy jiggled in her chair opposite Little Barry, her legs swinging above the floor. Anne faced me across the round table. I mumbled a short blessing and reached for the serving spoon.

"Dan, Little Barry has something he wants to say before we start, don't you, honey?"

"Oh, good, son, let's hear it."

Little Barry gathered himself, bringing his hands together over his salad. He took a deep breath. "I don't want to be 'Little Barry' anymore." The kitchen clock hummed loud in my ears.

"You mean, honey, you'd like not to be called 'Little Barry' any longer," Anne clarified for him.

"Yes, Mom, like I said."

"I like Little Barry." Wendy sounded confused for a moment, and then she stuffed her mouth full of bread.

Life can pull away from you like petals of a flower plucked one at a time from the stalk. As long as one leaf is hanging on, you can believe in survival. I'm not much at analogies. Barry must have shrunk as I grew up, is all I can make of those years after he came back. He was gaunt and bony, the T-shirts hanging from his shoulders like shopping bags, while my arms and torso corded with muscle from construction jobs. I grew in other ways too, learning how to talk with doctors, lawyers, social workers and military ombudsmen. The harder I fought for Barry's health benefits, the less he seemed to care. Days, he spent out back. As his rants and ramblings filled our house, Little Barry grew skeptical about the Big Barry I reminisced about: math whiz, star scout, double-A shortstop. Barry became a collage of stories and shadows. My big brother, Little Barry's namesake and uncle. Whenever I watched my son brush his teeth, I thought of my brother singing the Ipana song.

Sitting on the ground where the pine needles have fallen and spread their prickly carpet to the edge of the field, I consider my son's request and wonder who I am to grant or to refuse it. I've been loyal to my brother since birth, and even though he's become a different person, I still know and love him, as he was, as he is. It's a contradiction and sorrow I live with, and what should I expect from my son? What's in a name isn't everything, but it's a lot. Barry himself would understand the kid changing his name. He knew better than me what you could change and what you had to live with as is. I think about being known as a grower and drug dealer, what could be in files of the law that brand me. They won't say what kind of brother I am, or father.

The breeze bends the high bank of pine boughs. Clear sky reaches all the way to kingdom come, where Barry imagined a blue peace. The marijuana plants flicker among the rowdy weeds like bright green battle flags. The first one fights me, and then, wrapped halfway 'round my hand, the stem jolts out of the ground, trailing a cap of soil and its tap root. I wade into the field.

My son already sees a picture for himself, and I hope it blesses and keeps him through what happens and who he becomes. I really do.

SIGNS

R ONNIE pulled the long dirty thing from his shoulder pack
and laid it out on the sand. I knew what it wasn't. A
snake. A rubber hose. A connecting tube for electrical wires.

"Ain't that some shit." Ronnie knew what it was all right,
but in the way he tossed it on the ground I had the feeling he
wasn't going to pick it up again. "So, you're first two guesses
are way off; number three, and you're out!"

My father practiced this ritual that used to piss off my
mother no end. On the anniversary of his return home from
Saigon, he'd head out to his retreat in the woods with a six-
pack of Chinese beer and be gone all day. When I was a kid he
wouldn't let me go with him, and he had a way of looking at
my mother so she wouldn't want to go with him. I remember
the echoes of wood splitting and the steady whack-whack of
the axe. It would be dark when he came to the back door. For
seventeen years it was the same picture: Dad's hair matted
over his forehead, covering half his ears, red-rimmed eyes,
a shot kind of expression in his face, his broad shoulders

sagging under the sweat-caked and clinging T-shirt. At least I knew school would be over and summer would officially begin the next morning. On the eighteenth anniversary, Dad didn't come in from the woods.

The media center covered half of our family room wall, and as brightly colored images of Humvees and tanks flashed by in the distance, little children ran across a chewed-up street at the near edge of the screen. A crisp British accent described the battle field. The children were the new refugees: barefoot, "tattered and small" lost among the bombed-out buildings of the settlement. They caught the attention of the camera for those quick seconds of the report before the studio back-drop of the Chicago skyline wiped across the screen and the ad dropped in: an egg-shell colored Lexus cruising across the Golden Gate.

I thought of my father as a young man, maybe just after his sophomore year in college, two months before he decided to let the draft catch up with him. He'd be downshifting into the entrance ramp, pressing the accelerator mid-way, dropping the rear end into the belly of the first curve and then slipping into the fast lane, one foot on the clutch, the other on the gas, synchronizing, he'd aim the old Indian head into the bulls eye of the long suspended corridor to the other side. Vroom!

The doctor had to use the three-cell flashlight to follow the path out into the woods. He let me go with him, but I could sense his anxious doubts. He was the only man my father really talked to, and the doc's slow progress down the path seemed to confirm something only he suspected. He wept when the light beam showed what my father had done to himself with the axe. It was a "decisive" slash, he said, as if to no one. The light danced away and we found the way back to the house by zeroing in on its glow through the new leaves of the close growing trees. He told my mother of Dad's tragic accident with the axe. "Bled out," was how he put it.

Ronnie grinned at me as if he'd just gotten away with murder. "Go ahead, if you're wrong the third time, you own it."

A formation of choppers leaned into the azure sky and I looked up at them as much to make sure they weren't targeting us as to wish I were on one of them. I looked back down at the child's intestine, knowing in that way you wish you didn't, exactly what it was. I felt like wrapping it around Ronnie's grimy neck and choking him with it. Then he'd own it, just like he did now, only it would own him back.

It was a scene that returned whenever it wanted to. Nothing distracted me from it for long. It was the TV picture I couldn't flick off. When my wife bounced into the room with good news about the baby's tooth, or when the bigger kid dragged me outside to play ball, I could reflect the excitement, the goodness, but I couldn't feel it. I could touch my bigger kid's perfect little rib cage, but it was someone else's hands making the contact. I could hear myself shout encouragement; words of affection floated out of my mouth like bubbles, and they popped silently above his head across the lawn.

The officer asked me to touch my nose with the index finger of my right hand. I felt silly and resolute at the same time. Walking a straight line, lifting my foot, stretching out my arms, eyes closed. Okay. I knew he wouldn't nab me. DUI. Fine, maybe headlines on page two, but not tonight. I learned one thing in the army. You can be drunk but you can act like you are not. The officer shot his light into my eyes from very close range.

"You passed all the exercises," he said, "but you're drunk as a skunk. Get back in the car and drive straight home. I'll be following you."

I could see what my father got out of splitting wood. You really have to let the maul fly; visualize the head driving all the way through the center of the target to the ground. If the round sections were dry enough, the wood popped open with a satisfying crack, but greener wood or a long knot can stop a maul with a dull thud. Breaking through to the ground then becomes a contest of wills. A couple of hours, whaling away, swinging a ten-pounder, wrapping and rewrapping your hands around the hard oak shaft, can be hard labor, exhausting. What starts out as fairly straight forward and rote technique morphs into a game of hitting the sweet spot where it lurks within easy reach, disguised in radiating rings from core to cambium. It stares up at you like a golf ball. You can hear it dare you: "hit me, little man, go ahead, hit me."

My wife knows the story about what happened to my dad, but she didn't know him. She doesn't like my wood splitting routine much more than my mother liked my father's, even though she claims there's no connection between the story and me in her mind. I wonder if there's any connection to two wood burning fire places and me splitting wood in her mind, but I don't bring it up often. It's a losing argument all the way round.

I watch the news programs, the talk shows, the staged panel discussions that feature experts and pundits. It's entertaining sometimes, and always depressing. I must like to be entertained by depression or else I would spend evenings doing something else, I guess. My father hung out with his buddies at a joint near the bowling alley where his high school team was a perennial league leader in strikes and spares. I think they also lead the league in draft beer consumption after hours. They all joined the U.S. Army after graduation, all except my father who won a scholarship at a small liberal arts college in New York State. My mother couldn't tell you where it was, exactly. She met him at a homecoming dance for new vets, the closing act at the bankrupt bowling alley.

I decided a long time ago not to spend my life locked inside my own head. I'd tell my story. I'd lie with my woman all night and share my dreams. I'd go out into the world and bring back good news. If I had to fight in a war, I'd keep my morals, be proud of my country, myself. You know, do good things. Even if I ended up right back where I came from, I wouldn't judge it as a failure to make the world a better place: just the opposite. What better place to better than your home town? I still think that way, most of the time.

"You gotta walk the talk," Ronnie used to chant when we were on patrol. "Talk tough, walk tough." If you learn what that's about, exercise it like a mantra, like muscle memory, it's hypnotic. It gets you through tough times and out of tough places, but when you're in easy times and places, talking tough makes a big echo that swallows you. I learned one thing in my two years in college; I could talk the talk. In the army I learned to walk it. When I'm splitting wood, it all comes together sometimes.

I see that intestine lying on the dirty sand. There's a hum in my eyes, and far off across the phantasmagoria of this place, a tall willowy figure swings a silent axe. Snowflakes big and white as Frisbees fall through the bare trees. I know these visions and these woods are competing realities in my head, and I line up the eye of a fat chunk of maple with the blunt tip of the maul. I can purge the face of that kid looking for his guts if I swing hard enough. And, I can still walk the talk so that if I ever see Ronnie again, I can spit in his eye and go home.

A FATHER'S WILL

A LLEGHENY Road cut off at a ninety degree angle from
Rose Road, and after running over two steep hills and
a swamp-bottomed gully, climbed to the crest of the long
east-west ridge before descending past the farm's southern-
most pasture lane where it disappeared into the Wyoming
County woods. The house stood on the ridge. A long row of
poplar trees shielded the north side of the house. Between
the front porch, its roof propped up by four bowed ten by six
beams, and the road, a low scraggly hedge caught the brown
and yellow leaves blown about by the northwest wind. An
old maple nursed her scars at the corner of the lawn where
the cracked sidewalk and dirt shoulder became the widest
mud puddle on the place when rain came.

Across the road and half way down the hill from the
farm house, the milk house window filled with yellow light.
It was visible from the top of the first hill where I turned onto
Allegheny. It was as if it had always been exactly like that,
the scene painted against the moonless evening. I could have
been a sixteen-year-old coming home on the school bus from a

Friday night basketball game instead of the guy driving home alone fifteen years later.

I wondered if Dad had ever changed the bulb in the milk house. My Volvo fit easily onto the wide shoulder across the road from the house. I turned off the engine and headlights and sat in the dark. November hardened the trees and bare hedges. A gust of wind shook the car. Faint strains of light warmed the bay windows of the house, and I knew supper was cooking. I felt the pull between wanting to go down to the barn to find Dad and slipping around to the back door to surprise Mother.

Dad didn't hear me coming between the rows of stanchions. Any sounds I made were consumed in the groaning and munching of ninety cows and the steady chunka-chunka-chunka of the electric milking machines that created a suction perfect as a calf's mouth, more productive than the best farmer's hands. I spotted Dad near the end of the row of Holstein buttocks. He leaned in under the mass of the black and white cow's bulging rib cage; his head laid tight against her hide, his engineer cap pulled low, his thermal cotton shirt rippled in the design of his own rib bones. He pulled and squeezed her teats to the music of the milking machines; his target, a stainless steel pail. I stood as close as I could without stepping across the gutter behind the cows.

"Still doing it the old fashioned way, huh Dad?" He didn't lift his head or miss a beat.

"Lo, boy. She's got some mastitis. Been up to the house?"

"Just got here, thought maybe you'd want to talk before supper. You don't write many letters, you know."

He pulled and squeezed the two back teats. His hand muscles stretched into his fingers. Under his shirt sleeves the cords and muscles of his forearms flexed sympathetically with the milky spray of one teat, two teat, one teat.

"Never talk much while milking."

"No news there."

"Nope." Then by some signal he felt in the cow's teats or sensed in the shifting of her hind legs, the shape and size of knotted tree limbs, he let go the teats, grabbed the pail handle in his left hand, stood, ran his right hand hard along the cow's side and reached out to me in a grip that nearly pulled me into the gutter. Dad's teeth shone through his salt and pepper stubble and the dry-gulch creases of his face broke open from the corners of his mouth all the way up to his eyes. "Glad you finally made it home, I was beginning to wonder if I had a son or just the memory of one."

"Sorry about that."

"No apologizing. Let's go wash up for supper. Your mother's probably cooked enough for two suppers."

He was right, the dining table was spread end to end. There wasn't a dish of corn, peas, or beets, potatoes or greens that hadn't been grown on the farm. The flank steak was cut from a steer Dad bought at auction, and the strawberries for shortcake had ripened in the patch behind the house.

"Bet you can't eat like this in Boston." Mom was proud of the table, but matter-of-fact, too.

"Nobody eats like this, yogurt and tofu are big, now." I ate until eating was reflex, hunger long gone. Dad sopped up gravy and greens juice with a homemade biscuit and washed it down with a cup of warm pasteurized milk. Mother simply enjoyed my gluttony. She watched me throughout the meal, poking absentmindedly at her plate. Her house dress hung on her broad shoulders and the V cut by her dark blue apron seemed to pin her straight up in her chair.

"You've got great posture, Mom. How do you do it?"

"Thought I'd be withering away to a shadow? I'm not

preparing to lie in any grave soon, though your father's talking like we're meeting our maker momentarily."

"Now, that's not true, Floss, that's not so. I've just been reviewing the future, so to speak, and dying just happens to be out there."

"Behind every tree, to hear you go on."

"Well, if you can look around this farm at two generations of hard work and hard living and add up all those days that come to the day we're sitting, right here, eating like we was at the last supper, you tell me what you come up with."

She answered him, blending kindness with a kind of reprimand. He said he'd been left with too much work and too little help, no sons who'd stay home, no daughters who'd bring it upon themselves to marry local boys. I looked at the wall facing me. The framed high school graduation photos of my brother and two sisters looked back. Bill grinned, Suzanne's impressionistic profile feigned nostalgia, Caroline's long blond hair shaded her angular serenity. I'd never liked my picture, and I liked it less now. I couldn't imagine Mom or Dad looking at it and seeing anyone other than the wide-eyed jerk about to trip across the stage. They had stopped talking. They must have been waiting for me to chime in.

"Don't apologize for not listening to us, Dave. We probably weren't saying anything to interest you, but that's how it goes after awhile."

"Judd, you've been just this way ever since I met you."

"S'pose it's true. Nothing I can do about it now, either."

"No one asked you to, dear. It would just be nice if our long away from home son could enjoy his short visit."

"You having a bad time, so far, Dave?"

"No, Dad. Really, there's nothing either of you has to do special for me. Being here is special enough, it's been a long time, and I know there's a lot to say, and nothing, too, of course." They looked at me intently in some sort of rediscovery. I felt a little like a ministerial candidate for the village church. They nodded in unison as if I had passed the test of being who they thought I would be.

"My, you've certainly grown up a lot, David Gibson McGee. You can probably out-talk and out-think both of us, but you're too much of a gentleman."

"Nonsense, Floss, the only thing he can out-do us at is livin', and that's only because he got a late start on us." We laughed suddenly, and then Dad said, "besides, you should call us Judd and Floss. That Dad and Mom stuff is from another life, and I should stop calling you, son, especially when you're not around. Don't make much sense, but I do it, you know. My first son, Billy, had a name, but somehow my second son is just my son. Maybe because I knew you'd be the last one."

Mother looked at him in a doubtful wonder, tears in her eyes. Dad stared at the framed photos. "And the girls never had names in my head either, just, my girls, and if I saw much of them now, I wonder if their names would come to me easier. Maybe names are for grandchildren. I can rattle those off like the days of the week. Not their birthdays, no, by God, if it weren't for Floss, I'd miss 'em all."

"Judd, how about some tea? Coffee for you, Dave?" She was already half way to the kitchen. I looked at Dad as he slid his chair around so he could cross his legs. He faced me more directly and continued his whimsical talk, but after a few lines the reminiscences trailed off and he leaned toward me.

"Before I forget, we've got to discuss a couple of things regarding my will."

"Your letter didn't say much specific, except being the executor makes me think about things I'd rather not think about."

"Well, I could get somebody else to do it."

"That's not what I mean. I'll do it because you want me to, besides, I'm sure you know what you're doing."

"Well, the will's all set unless you want to change your life and come back to run the farm like I used to hope you would. My father got it ready for me, and even though I wanted to high-tail it for somewheres else, you know how that story worked out."

Mom brought in a small pot of tea for Dad and cup of coffee for me. She cleared the rest of the dishes and returned to the kitchen. Dad kept talking as if we'd had a brief intermission.

"My father was hard-minded clever about what he wanted for his years of hard work, and for his son. And, I knew, being his only son, that I'd have to make up my mind certain, if I wanted something different bad enough, and he had me before I knew it, and I guess I didn't mind, 'cause I married your mother, and worked and built every day, just like he did, and like I'm doing still, and will do until I can't do it no more.

"Maybe I thought about going off to a place like New York or Montreal to live and become something I wasn't, but I guess too, that I pretty much knew who I was and what I could do. I can only imagine what you do. Don't know a whole lot about business, but I like to think I do now and then.

"The will's drawn up and fixed, all right. We can get it in town tomorrow, but there's a few things I couldn't put in the damned thing, and I'll have to talk about them with you, private and confidential, for at least as long as your mother and I live."

I wanted to know what he was talking about, but he got up and stretched his arms toward the ceiling and retreated to the bathroom. I sat back and finished my luke-warm coffee. The ride began catching up with me, and the kitchen sounds of dishes, the refrigerator door muffling open and shut, relaxed me into a doze. I started when Mom touched my shoulder, and by the time I had brushed my teeth and stripped off my clothes, I was wide awake. I could hear the murmurs and movements of my parents getting ready for bed, sharing the years of night-time ritual.

We had all closed our doors at night. Shut ourselves into our rooms as if they were smaller houses within the big house where we kept our vulnerabilities and our breathing to ourselves. Now, the doors of my sisters and brother stood open. Our parents' night life circulated among them, touching I knew not what, but there was a benign affection in the steady flow of breathing, a peculiar kind of peace. I lay under the hand-me-down quilt from my grandmother and wondered if Judd and Floss kept us all alive, living there in perpetuity, with their harmonic breathing. Did memories of Notre Dame, a rusty horse shoe, the wall of mystery novels represent us in their dreams?

Dad came in from the barn around 8 a.m. He'd been milking since dawn. He washed up and sat next to me at the kitchen table. The barn odor came alive in the warm kitchen.

"Cold, bitter, so far. Looks like it'll stay that way, too. I thought you'd be skipping breakfast."

"It's just toast and coffee, usually, but Mom's eggs and bacon could get to be a habit real quick."

"Good. Soon's I get my second cup, I'll shower and we can head for Batavia. Won't take long." He sat for a few minutes, just looking out the window over the sink where the top halves of trees and the low sky were framed. "We can talk in the car," he said, and downed the coffee.

Dad had always driven fast. He aimed his Oldsmobile

at a target on the horizon and sank into the seat as if speed itself had hold of him, then he relaxed. His calloused left hand rested on top of the steering wheel, and he waved and pointed with the other hand like a tour director. His curiosity about farm equipment kept his eyes sweeping the passing countryside for combines and pickers he hadn't noticed on his previous trips to town. With winter approaching, most of the newer machinery was idle or covered, but he made sure to mention the names of the farmers who neglected to protect their machines.

"Well, I guess you didn't come all the way up here to inspect farm yards with your old man. I want to tell you a story, but I been keeping it to myself so long, I don't know if I can break it loose, just right. Something about time that stays the same in your mind, until you try to gather it together and bring it out, then, by God, you never know. Anyway, I hold 'em in the more I love 'em, the stories, the memories. But, if they don't come out, they aren't really stories, are they?"

"I see what you mean," I said, "I guess you have to decide if you want it to be a story, before you tell it, cause then, anything can happen to it."

"Yeah, well, you'll get to do something with this one. It's about a girl I loved a long time ago. Before I met your mother. She was a city girl, long, silky legs, soft hair and a real jaunty gait. I'd only grown up with farmers' daughters, and you know that story. So, Milly was her name, she looked like a queen to me. She had money from somewhere and all I had to do was go along and help her spend it. We went to Niagara Falls for just one night, but it turned into a week. My daddy nearly disowned me. He coulda done it, too, literally. When I dragged myself into the barn he acted like I was a cob web, brushed me off, kept on milking and doing chores. It was late June; we were haying, and he loved this farm, so anything that came between it and him made him mad as hell. He'd been working hard to keep the place in shape for me, and that's the day he finally burst out with it. Well, I didn't know what to say.

"I just wanted to grow up and get away for awhile, see places, taste different women, you know those pin-ups at the feed mill looked pretty good in those days. This Milly, in fact, fit the whole bill. I still dream about her once-in-awhile like it was yesterday, her riding me around the bed. Sorry, you can leave that part out."

"No need to apologize, Dad." I felt uncomfortable and kept looking out the window.

"No? Well, dammit, it didn't last. I found myself back here trying to sweat that woman out of my skin. Threw some powerful racks of hay that summer, I'll say. Met your mother at a cattle auction in August and took the plunge into an early marriage. It was so fast I still go over to the wedding picture on the sideboard to make sure the boy with his arm around Floss is me."

The outskirts of Batavia broke the rolling farmland. Dingy frame houses stood on lots cut from what used to be fertile bottom land. The old farmhouses hunkered among the smaller capes and ranches, and even though a few of them were fixed up and painted like mansions, they looked lonely, outdated. I looked at their floor to ceiling windows encased by wide, hand-hewn frames and imagined how a 19th century family might make a complete world for themselves inside. Dad stopped talking and when I glanced over at him, he nodded a couple of times and creased a smile at me.

The lawyer greeted us in his second story office that overlooked the downtown, decimated by urban renewal. Dad and I read copies of the will laid out on a thick slab of desk the lawyer called his "inheritance." He asked no questions and raised his voice just above a grunt as we shook hands and returned to the dark stairway to the street. I followed Dad to the bank where he deposited the will in the safety deposit box. He took an envelope from the box before he called the teller, and then we headed for the car and aimed for home.

Batavia slipped behind us, and Dad reached into his red and black checked jacket to pull out the envelope. He swung it easily toward me and I took it almost reflexively, feeling its unexpected weight. The envelope itself was blank.

"I want you to keep it until the time comes to give it to Milly. I wrote it a long time ago, but it says what I never knew how to say to her, what I should have said at the time. And, if you decide not to accept the farm as stated in the will, then this memory of mine will mean even more than it already does. I'm trusting you to take care of it, regardless."

I assumed the envelope contained Milly's address, or directions on how to locate her. What if she died before Dad? I looked at his bony profile, his deep-set eye socket, looking almost detached from his cheek bone. But he looked good, creasing into a smile that widened into a big happy grin. What was he thinking, or seeing in his mind's eye? Milly, horseback riding, Floss, sliding through the wedding night curtains in the half-light of nakedness? A new combine?

"Well, there it is. That's the story, and now it's yours, too."

We turned fast onto Allegheny, stones and gravel flying against the wheel wells. Though it was early afternoon, the sunless sky seemed ready to fade entirely. From the top of the second hill I spotted the pale glow in the milk house window. Dad saw it too.

"I'll be damned if the one thing I can't remember to do around here is to turn out that light! Must have had that same bulb going for near forty years. Maybe you can take care of that for me, son."

"I'll try," I laughed. "I'll sure try."

WHERE I AM

I'M in love with your husband. How women come up to me and say it so blithely, in the store, at parties, the post office. They mean it as some sort of compliment, I suppose, trying to make me feel good about all the time he spends over, under, and inside them. The time I wouldn't give a tick to if it weren't for them reminding me that my husband handles their private parts like a vintner tests grapes for ripeness and rot.

He's got wonderful hands, I know. I watch his fingertips skin shrimp, parting the thin fingernail-like shells along the belly seam, flicking the flaccid legs apart, slipping the meat from the last hold of the flexy fan tail. As he washes bunches of spinach, he has a way of shaking the leaves dry without the use of the spinner.

I'm in love with my husband too, as it turns out, even though he spends long days at the office listening to their complaints, caressing their sore tummies, parting the waves of their thighs to contemplate currents of the red sea.

But Geselle might mean it differently than Colleen Gamble or Midge Martinelli. Geselle holds her hands at her chest, heels and palms pressed together. "I'm in love with your husband," she sighs theatrically as we face each other beside her waxy, red Audi. The parking lot stretches out around Harmony Hills Mall, and I squint into the blazing reflections of a hundred windshields, avoiding eye contact with her.

"He's from the old school, you know, Madeleine. He knows how to communicate with a woman, if you get my drift."

I hate the way people pick up stupid fragments of vernacular. Geselle's what's drifty, and I do get it.

"I just couldn't see any other doctor."

"I know how you feel, Geselle." I laugh lightheartedly and shade my eyes to search rows of twinkling car roofs for my van.

"You don't know how fortunate you are, Madeleine, to live with a man like that."

"Well, I don't live with a man like that; I live with the man himself." I know I shouldn't have said it, but there's only so much baiting a wife can take. Still, bad manners on my part.

"You look good, Madeleine," she says, her flaky blues focused on the swath of gray, half curled over my temple. "Healthy."

"Oh, I can't afford not to be, with such a wonderful husband to keep up with." I smile, biting my lower lip, feeling suddenly like a woman struggling with a congestive heart.

Doug and I rarely talk medicine. It's one of those things that we tried early on and just found unsatisfying. He does say at times that he's just a high-priced custodian, intimate with the nooks and crannies of other people's basements. He's delivered over 3,000 babies, and he refuses to do abortions under normal circumstances.

We sleep in our queen-sized bed, back-to-back against

each other, making an embryo of safe, warm feeling between us. When he leaves for a night call, my back gets sticky cool, and I half awaken to fish for the covers, to pull one of Doug's pillows inside my arms to cuddle.

He says our not having children doesn't bother him, but it seeps into my abdomen while I'm dropping back to deep sleep, that emptiness without words, that condition Jane Austen might allude to as *barren*. I knead and press the form into something less abject. *Fallow*. Sometimes a baby name we used to consider from those pink and blue Signets comforts me. Abigail, Lucinda, Hope.

There are other women like me who work at jobs or professions they like—I'm at the Institute of Art in town—who live busy and committed lives, who seldom fall into pits of self-doubt. But I'm sure sometimes they do doubt and wish and regret. That's when the Geselles get the scent. Behind the cunning smiles and friendly chatter, they're licking your ice cream.

Vulnerability is my worst fault. I swear sometimes I'm a clumsy seventh-grader wearing faded tights, cracking my toes in Capezios along the wall bar in Miss Celestine's dance studio. The heat is off for class. The draft stings my damp crotch. I feel transparent.

I catch myself staring at the framed poster hanging on the wall in my office. It's from the Godiva Retrospective Exhibit, Avignon, 1992. She's half turned toward the abstract image of the cathedral, her blond cascade of hair fingers her waist above the cleavage of her buttocks as she straddles the horse.

The morning paper lies open across my computer keyboard. I routinely scan the news before concentrating on the art and movie review section. I've taken to the public relations work of linking the arts community with business in the sponsorship of arts events. It's sensible and satisfying, but today, the front page has not been flipped aside.

The story of a woman, whose dead baby was discovered by her own nine-year-old son while he was out looking for a stray cat in the woods behind their rented trailer, faces me. In the queasy distance separating erotic imagery on the wall and the nauseating news story, my sense of equilibrium wavers. I try not to imagine the baby itself. I reconsider the mother's statement to the police, like, she "didn't know" she was pregnant. The husband's unemployed, hasn't "yet been to see his wife in jail." My mind runs to circumstances I've never experienced. A deadbeat husband. A disheveled trailer on a back-country road. A son who stopped being a joy a long time ago. I feel tears cloud my eyes, but I hold on, staring at a foggy Godiva.

Doug comes home late after I've eaten the leftover shrimp and linguine. He opens the refrigerator, and I trace the portrait of his fine features in the half-tones of the light. He closes the door and turns empty-handed to me at the counter. I can see the dusty tiredness in his eyes, the slight rounding of his shoulders under the smudged white shirt, where sweat and stain marks have dried into the fabric from the day's routine exertion and splatter.

"I'm not hungry," he says. "You look tired. Maybe we should just go to bed."

"Thanks," I try to smile. "At least you didn't tell me how healthy I look."

He puts his hand on my arm and touches my cheek with his fingertips. "You look healthy, but tired, too."

"It's okay," I say, leaning against his chest, enfolding him in my arms, pressing my fingers into his shoulder blades. "I feel like I'm naked on a high wire and don't know how I got up here, or how I'll get down."

"An interesting position," he murmurs into my neck, and I feel his hands on my back, tender while firm. "You need some treatment," he decides, and those hands guide me through the hallway to the stairs and up to our bedroom where the evening air has brought the faint scent of mown grass through the windows.

We lie on our backs, dampness runs the crease of my breastplate to my navel. If the light were on, I could see the tight curls of Doug's chest hair clinging to my breasts, my flat belly. I listen to his breathing assume a soft rhythm and feel him gather into his own sleep. The impulse to poke him awake and ask him about Geselle nearly grabs my hands, but I dig in against it and measure the closeness between us, the place where I am.

There is something like a baby between us. A third thing we make without naming it or putting it into vulnerable reality. He must be carrying it around with him. Why else would women be in love with him? I think about the comfort he must give and receive, and I feel myself letting go into sleep.

THRUWAY

R UDY lay still, naked on the wide bed. At four in the morning the steady whine of truck tires from the highway was broken by the intervals of snoring let off by his wife next to him.

Why he'd stayed on this long was the early morning question revisited, why he'd thought it was a good idea to accept the deed, the mortgage, the barn, the cows, the works. His father wasn't retiring to Arizona for the weather, and the farm wasn't what you'd call a break even proposition, but it was there, and he was there, and what else did he have in mind then, anyway.

Mindy rolled over on her side and let out a long , deep sigh. He had two hours ahead to doze on and off through the loaded questions of repetition.

You can believe you can make changes later and all the while remain stuck in place. The new interstate would slice his farm nearly perfectly in half and with right-of-ways and the proposed exit ramp not a mile west, his best bottom land would be cut off from the house and barn. He took the developer's first offer on that part of the farm, fearing outright condemnation that might be his next best offer. Selling the herd was more painful than the measly sum collected. Even now, he lapsed into memories of the cattle trucks leaning out of the barn yard, weighed down with his healthy cows and his bright beautiful heifers. It was as if he'd become an old man in the course of an afternoon.

No one ever tells you these things, that your stupid cows really do get you up in the morning, that the long low fields of your sweat and heartache really are the pastoral dreams of your livelihood. The future shortens up pretty quick when you cash in. What's the point in thinking about it?

•   •   •

The old two-lane road brought the mail and the milk truck. Each day Rudy timed his progress around the place on those two reliable events. Truck by ten, mail by two. He could finish the milking and clean up the pens before the truck arrived to pump out the cheese from his 600 gallon tank. Joking with Clem about what kind of cheese they'd make from his milk was something to look forward to, and while he tinkered with the milking machines at the faucet near the milk house door, Clem would lean against the underside of the tanker and smoke his long Pall Malls, rain or shine. Rudy never smoked around the barn, but he trusted Clem not to start any fires. A few cars usually glided by while he talked outside the milk house and the lazy waves from their drivers were like signal passages of time itself: nice and easy all's right with the world, and you, too.

It wasn't so much that he missed Clem or the work of milking the cows, slip-sliding out to the barn to deal with big animals so docile that you could punch and swear at them without causing a fuss. It was something else. Something that crept up on him and slowly stole his action, his will to act, his reason, if he could name it, for being who he was where he was, for to be no one no where was not as far as he could imagine.

Mindy rolled onto her back and in a snatch of breath eased into a steady snore. He got up then and stumbled the few steps to the high-backed arm chair by the windows. He lay back and watched the sky's low glow hover over the highway truck depot. Every year it seemed they expanded. From a rest stop to a truck depot, a place for a dozen carriers to pull over, to a park designed for hundreds of tractor trailers at a time, firing up, cooling down, droning away all hours, all meaning of day or night, marking all time by the gallon, gross weight.

Rudy had watched his neighbors settle up and leave one by one. And, the ones who stayed shut down little by little and died somehow. He'd been to the funerals, and he'd go to more as they came. But the road would stay, outlast all the living and be waiting for the unborn, the uninitiated lovers of tires, engines, freight, wages. He saw long rows of corn undulating to the horizon of trees. Black muck offering up onions, half-buried mushroom huts hunkering in the daze. When the fox used to hunt during the night while the chickens huddled against the back corner of the coop and clucked quiet. He missed that fox, so stealthy and sleek, not taking luck for granted or risking his life for a hen.

Rudy took the truck driving job out of spite he thought at the time, but he actually needed the steady pay-check. When the phone rang on Saturday mornings for the Buffalo to Boston run he felt defeated.

He heard the ring before it rang. He pulled on his jeans before he found them on the back of the bathroom door. He tasted Mindy's sleeping mouth before he kissed her good-bye. The sixteen-wheeler groaned into motion before he climbed into the cab, and as the sun crawled out of the Atlantic far to the east, the road woke in bleak shades of gray, and Rudy raised his hand to the window neither in farewell or welcome, a wave of static proportions giving everything to everybody and nothing to nobody.

NATURAL CAUSES

The spleen weighs 260 grams.

O UR house had one of the first poured concrete foundations
in the village, and a handful of men showed up just to
watch the event. Dirk McCabe was busy all afternoon sluicing
concrete from his truck into the lumber frames outlining our
basement walls. That July evening with the hay fields rich
in haze and the scent of alfalfa blanketing the air, the fresh
damp foundation of our new home cut such a deep shadow
into the ground that I was at a loss for words. I peered into the
symmetry and imagined one day soon when Roy would plumb
a work bench along the wall, and I would run clothes lines
under the beams to dry the wash during bad weather.

Roy pitched the tent under the maples that lined the
boundary of Burdick's field. Beside the tent, he strung a
hammock. One afternoon I crept through the long grass
down to its swelled stillness, wanting to surprise Roy as
he took in the crickets and the slight cooling of the air
under the broad reach of the maple limbs. As I reached the
head of the hammock, Roy jumped from behind the near
tree and scared me. We laughed at how he'd wrapped up

some old building tarps to resemble a body lounging in the hammock. At night, lying naked on the army cots under the taut canvas roof, we talked in whispers of how each room of the downstairs would connect to the next room to form a rectangular perimeter around all sides of the basement stairway, front door foyer, and rear entryway. Our living room floor would be shiny oak, and the bay windows would look out on the very row of trees we lay under. We could see it together, the vision keeping us awake.

•   •   •

Roy and I drove the Dodge coupe through the foothills of the Alleghenys and the little villages and crossroads settlements that grew up along the fast-flowing creeks, where mills and factories had found easy hydro-power during the last century. Most of the mills had fallen down. Deserted, forlorn, their turbines and machinery salvaged or stolen, their furniture and rusted benches heaped in overgrown driveways to rot alongside the dilapidated structures. A few antique shops occupied old storefronts in Varysburg. "Old" was not popular then, and prices were dirt cheap. In spite of our desire for the new, Roy and I loaded the coupe with old furniture, some of it in pieces, and strapped bed frames, headboards and side tables to the top of the car and across the hood. On the slow, winding drive home, we talked about refinishing and arranging our treasures. By the time we pulled into our narrow driveway on Prospect Hill Avenue, we'd already agreed on what we still needed to complete our collection. In this manner, we furnished the living room, bedroom and sewing room during our very first year. It made financial sense, too. We could drive a late model car, and Roy could afford a couple of new suits for his job at the bank. With the savings account and the plan for two children, the house was just right for the life we would live there, together.

I got a job working for Doc Wells, who was county coroner at the time, elected unopposed on the Republican ticket. For what they paid him to go out in all conditions, at all hours, he could have bought a new raincoat. I scheduled Doc's maternity patients right along with the broken-down grandparents of some of the pregnant newlyweds. I became the accountant and did just about whatever else was needed. That's how I got into transcribing Doc's coroner's cases from his scratchy notes and the Dictaphone recordings he made on Sunday afternoons. The records of how people's lives ended seemed to me to say so much about life itself, and so little. A man could survive a harrowing birth, a malnourished childhood, farm mishaps, flu, dog bites, graduate high school, marry, inherit a farm, father six children, make a go of it and die suddenly at the ripe old age of thirty-five. It's always 'sudden' or 'unexpected', by natural causes. The pain and agony of loss is natural too, I suppose.

Often, it was somebody I knew or used to know. Mildred Sampson, stroke. Harriett Lyons, heart failure. Manfred Santelli, complications from diabetes. Growing up, I shared the same teachers' lessons with them, sang along with them to the same hymns in church. I typed their names under the official headings of the county coroner's office and remembered their faces.

I could blaze through a pile of coroner's reports in a single evening of typing. I was fast in my school typing course, but now I hit top speed on Doc's office Corona. The keys leapt at my finger tips; it was as close as I could get to playing the piano. Eyes squinting, fingers dancing, I focused on descriptive details I would later try to forget. The coroner's cases made the *Batavia Daily News* for the record, but if they were gory enough, they got stories and pictures, too. I wouldn't want to be a pathologist, or a reporter either, for that matter. So many stories are haunting, and senseless.

This two-year-old Puerto Rican boy was said to have a fever. The night prior to admission to the Emergency Room of St. Jerome Hospital on 1/30/47, was given aspirins, and apparently felt better.

Aspirins, for gosh sakes! They should have called Doc first. I would never treat a baby so casually. Certainly not our own.

The body is that of a well-developed, slender two-year-old White male, 34" in body length, weighing approximately 60 pounds... The scalp is covered with thick, dark brown hair. The irises are brown. The pupils are round, regular, and fixed in mid-position. No discharge exudes from the nose, ears, or mouth. The chest and abdomen are of normal contour. The external genitalia, upper and lower extremities, and back do not reveal any gross pathologic change.

I pictured the boy and his deep brown smiling eyes, his head cradled in the crook of his mother's arm. I thought of the scalpel and kept typing.

The body is opened ventrally in the midline from the suprasternal notch to the symphysis pubis. Upon opening the abdomen, it is found filled with abundant, thick, turbid, yellow, somewhat rancid-smelling liquid material associated with multiple, fibrinopurulent adhesions, which mat loops of contiguous small and large bowel to one another and also cover the omental apron, which is

also moderately indurated and reddened.
  Findings: Appendicitis.
  Peritonitis, purulent, generalized.

•   •   •

The walls and roof beams went up in one day of barn raising hoopla. From near six a.m. to dark, Roy and his brothers and their buddies from high school, the ones who got back from the war, put up the frame of the whole house. When the sun settled into the thick haze that night, the bushy evergreen nailed to the front peak stood proudly in the fading light. We tied the tent flaps back to catch the slightest breeze. There was little talking as fatigue took Roy, and later me, into the dreamy sleep of the outdoors. Before I dropped off, I heard a faraway murmur, a voice too vague and distant to mean anything beyond the instant of thinking I had heard it, a sound a sleeping baby might make down the hall.

The kitchen was the only room that we miscalculated. Somehow the entryway from the back porch door and the space for a large kitchen table got superimposed on the blueprints so that we were forced to decide whether to let the door open directly into the kitchen, right where the table would be, or to continue the inside wall so it would separate the entryway and the kitchen. That would make a smaller table necessary or eliminate a table entirely. The adjoining dining room was large and full of light from windows on the outside walls, so we had a side table for two built right into the kitchen wall near the counter. It would be good for breakfasts and quick lunches. Perfect for the two of us. It seemed like such a big problem, but Roy relied on my judgment to make the right decision, and he was really pleased with how things turned out.

Summer passed all too fast. The bank took a full nine-

and-a-half-hour day for Roy, and Doc Wells' office brimmed non-stop with minor complaints and no few serious cases of disease and injury. The relief I felt just making the ten-minute walk home at night would come at a rush as our house came into view over the crest of Prospect Hill Avenue.

The football season kept Doc busy with team physicals, injuries induced by violent body contact, and a variety of sprains and dislocations caused by the over-extension of physical capabilities at the wrong moment. What those moments became for the player were heroic acts of sacrifice for the cause. To me, they were a waste of good health and a snub at common sense. Doc loved football; he didn't miss a game, and he laughed that the healthier the player, the higher the risks he would take. There wasn't anything to do about it, he said, except to enjoy it and help out when needed. He was probably right, but I never changed my mind about football.

Halloween saw the completion of our front porch overhang, and I set the basket of MacIntoshes on a caned chair next to the fifty-pound pumpkin Roy carved into a grimacing clown face. The night turned unusually cold and rainy. All of a sudden we were contemplating winter and we chastised ourselves for the poor planning on the furnace hook-up. Fuel delivery was overdue, and the upstairs did not seem to gather heat from the living room fireplace like we had hoped.

Wrapped side-by-side in our double bed, covered by mother's hand-made quilts, we generated our own heat. It was the night of the first Halloween that I heard the distant murmur again, like the faraway cry of the summer, and I realized it was a wheeze deep inside Roy, a noise I could hear in every other breath or so, a sound that could have become a snore but didn't.

The day before Thanksgiving, our furnace and fuel supply

were up to snuff. The bank closed early the day before, and since Doc's office was normally closed Wednesdays, Roy and I found a rare time to work on the house. Roy walked home in the cold drizzle for lunch. He came into the back porch to remove his soggy shoes and unlined raincoat, soaked through to his suit coat. When he stood shoeless and shivering in the kitchen doorway, I asked him how many new accounts he'd opened. No accounts, but three builders loans and one refinanced home mortgage. Our little town was growing, it appeared.

Then, against my urging to change into dry clothes, Roy hugged me and sat at the small built-in, drop-leaf table wedged into the corner. He waited patiently for the barley soup and the tuna sandwiches to be served. He was stubborn about not changing until after lunch.

We spent the afternoon hanging drapes and curtains and cleaning the silt and dust made by the wall and ceiling construction. All that sawing and pounding seemed to go on forever, but now it was done, and we stood inside our new house like proud parents whose faith in each other just grew and grew. Roy's brothers wanted us to join the whole family at the homestead over in Oakfield, and we planned to go even though we hated to leave our place for the holiday.

Roy coughed on his way upstairs to change after lunch, and while we made busy with the decorating and cleaning chores, he coughed occasionally to clear his throat. The next day he said he felt like a wet pussy cat, but we went to his folks for Thanksgiving anyway. The following week started with a pile of coroner's reports and patient records mixed in with bills and receipts. Christmas cards began trickling in, too, and I had to sort things out before they overwhelmed the office. A pathologist's report and Doc's scribbled notes draped the typewriter. It was a good place to start.

Randolph Scruggs, Jr., age 20, of Lockport Road,

Oakfield, New York was trapped in the burning wreckage of a truck, which was operated by his brother-in-law, Timothy Bryan, 16, of 6312 North Byron Road, Elba, N.Y. The vehicle struck a tree head-on. The driver and the other passenger were thrown free and Randolph Scruggs, Jr., was trapped in the vehicle, which immediately caught fire. His body was severely burned and was brought to the morgue of St. Jerome's Hospital. An autopsy was done... which revealed the cause of death to be a ruptured aorta, due to fractured vertebra, and other multiple fractures. It is evident that the deceased died almost immediately after the accident and that the burning of his body took place postmortem.

CAUSE OF DEATH: Ruptured aorta and other injuries, as mentioned.

I held my breath up to the end, surmising he'd burned to death in the wreck. Horrible! Twenty, killed in a truck driven by kin on the way home to Thanksgiving dinner. While we were all eating turkey and stuffing, Scruggs burned. Mercy!

In those days, TB was common throughout the countryside. I sat behind my desk off the main waiting room with the window open a good crack for the circulation of fresh air even though I was shivering cold many times. I was afraid of catching it, or carrying it to Roy or the baby we started talking about. How Doc stayed healthy, I don't know. In medicine it's nothing but sickness and complaining you're taking into your life everyday. But he had an easy manner and a strong constitution. He was accepting and cheerful toward his patients, and they repaid him by coming back with all their medical needs, physical and mental. I learned from him to treat people simply, as though you truly cared about them. After awhile, I found myself caring without being overwhelmed by caring. Of course, I kept the accounts, so I knew who paid their bills and who didn't. To Doc, it didn't seem to matter. Since it was my job, it wasn't my inclination to forgive patients past three billings. You can't show these feelings in a small town, but my cheerfulness had a glint to it sometimes, I confess.

Our first winter lasted right through half of April. Easter Sunday came early, and it felt more like New Year's, but Roy wouldn't wear his overcoat, said his gray wool suit and new hat would be plenty. As the wind whipped snow around the eaves of our neat little barn, he was talking about breaking ground for the garden. In church, he coughed hard during the "Gloria Patri" and before the congregation sat, he gagged, stepped into the aisle and went down to the basement men's room. As soon as he left the pew, the idea that TB had followed me home from the office hit me. All those sick people, coughing without covering their mouths, spitting into handkerchiefs and Kleenex. Somehow, on my clothes, in my hair, I'd carried the bacteria up the hill, home. I felt like tearing my skin off.

Roy took a long time to die after Easter. The number of days wouldn't add up, but agony squares time, and Roy consumed his share. Time stretched out over day and night until there was no difference between light and dark. Each day was dawn and dusk until we buried him on cemetery hill north of the village following a nice service at the church.

Since then, I've come to learn that the long time he suffered was not long at all compared to how long I've been alone. Those long days and weeks and months, I tried to keep him comfortable, airing the corner room we'd papered and trimmed for the first baby, carrying trays of oatmeal and toast upstairs. Those waxy, bendable straws with every glass of juice, the cups of green mucus, sputum. I was caught up in cycles of coughing and carrying and caring, and I was relieved for him when it was over, even though, even though.

•   •   •

I never did need a lot of sleep, so I rise a few minutes before dawn to do my house work and get breakfast started. At night I shut the light off at eleven thirty and wait for my eyes to close. Propped on feather pillows in our four-poster bed, I listen for Roy's light step on the stairs, his humming in the bathroom, the water rushing through the pipes as he brushes his teeth and washes up. Sometimes I hear a cough in the baby's room. I call out: "Roy! Roy!"

Doc got the new Dictaphone as soon as they came out. A drug salesman brought it by for a special price, and Doc decided right away that he could use it. The pliable blue records slide into the top slot, and a hand-held microphone makes it easy for him to sit in his consultation room and record. After office hours, I listen to Doc's husky voice drone the facts and circumstances of the cases. The order and detail of death are distinct: fractured skull, smoke inhalation, massive trauma, chest wound. Brief inattention at the wrong time and place get you killed. We call them accidents, and just when you feel alert and in the thick of life, you can turn up in the obits anyway. Your heart stops while you sleep; a blood vessel bursts in your brain; your kidneys shut down; a bug overwhelms your immune system; cells mutate, rebel, metastasize. The clock winds down, the well runs dry. The last breath waits for you, wherever you may be, whatever you might be doing, whoever you think you are or will become.

So, after the patients clear the waiting room and slide off the porch benches for home, I plug in my ear phones and hammer away at the final acts of everyday lives. Most reports are paper-clipped with Daily News stories, photos of wrecks, fires, cops, graduation portraits. Certain stories stay with me, and I walk up the hill imagining my grip on the steering wheel the moment before the fatal curve whips at me, too fast, or I'm in the midst of conversation with Aunt Rebecca at the Greenwoods Inn when the chunk of beef lodges in my throat. What dumb gossip was it that choked me to death?

The victim had climbed a tree, accompanied by William Martin of 653 Red Mill Parkway, Batavia, N.Y., who was acting as an observer. The 16 gauge shotgun, which Novack was using, accidentally discharged while he was climbing down from the tree. The coroner investigated at the scene. He found the body leaning, in a sitting position, against the tree where the accident occurred. There was blood up in the tree in a crotch about 10 or 12 feet above the ground.

CAUSE OF DEATH: Hemorrhage, secondary to gun shot wound of the right thigh involving the right femoral artery.

To be that boy's mother all these years before getting the call. Like Roy, his life is a series of facts and feelings dependent on memory and devotion. Football, Honor Society, three younger brothers, first son. That damned Dictaphone.

•   •   •

Roy waits in the back hall for my return at night. No matter how late I am after doing the log book or transcriptions, he's there. Upstairs, I turn down the spread right away before I shuck my shoes and step into my slippers to go down to the kitchen. I brew two cups of chamomile tea, one with honey and lemon for Roy, the sweet tooth never leaves him, and just plain lemon for me. The cookies I bake Saturdays usually last the week, and we share three peanut butters and a macaroon.

I tell Roy about my day, leaving out the names he might know. The forty-year-old farmer's wife with MS, the feverish baby girl, allergies and rashes, fractures and colds. Most of the coroner's cases I keep to myself. Roy would rather hear about Doc fixing people up and the patients who call to cancel appointments for feeling better and wanting to save the fee. Roy was always a skinflint but good natured about it. I never accuse him of its putting him in an early grave and leaving me here to keep company with a cold cup of sweet tea. And, I don't say anything about my light-headedness, or the dizzy spells I get at the office.

Doc has stopped delivering babies. Sooner or later, he had to get on a regular schedule before he dropped, but I miss seeing the soon-to-be mothers and the procession of newborns. They inspire you with hope and a sense of timelessness. Now, being around the buzzing complaints of the elderly, pulling themselves up along the porch stair rails like wounded war veterans, makes me feel like a stream filling up with silt. I'll be a shallow trickle myself someday, and I watch our older patients shuffle ahead despite their stiffness and confusion.

Over the nights, time isn't so quick anymore. Roy is farther away than ever and when I wake from half-sleep to call, his name echoes from the dark stairwell. The feeling of Roy in the house has not been much comfort for a while, I admit. Have I been talking to myself all these years, believing it was Roy to comfort myself, only to awaken to that echo?

Do we know when it's gone, the answering voice, the cause for why we do what we do, stay where we stay, live like we live? I remember that hammock rounded out as if Roy languished there waiting just for me. I've been worried about how I will tell Roy. How can I keep calling to the silence? I also worry what the silence will want if I do stop, how I will keep it away, or how I will enter it.

•   •   •

Lying on my back now, wearing down from a rare and, so far, incurable blood disease, I listen to the locusts sawing away in the trees. It hasn't been below 85 degrees in two weeks, and, still, I'm cold. My memories seem to be competing. Patients' names and what they died of, drooling babies with their pink mothers, bits of comfort in conversation, news of loss and pain, that little evergreen nailed to our roof beam, my mother turning sideways in the saddle of her white faced stallion. I haven't outlived any of them, and there are some I would wish to, believe me.

In all my years with Doc Wells, I never heard of anyone actually dying of a broken heart. 'Natural Causes' turns up on most death certificates, and that's probably as close to a broken heart as the official record is likely to say. Doc is due to make a house call on me tonight, and I might ask him about it. Can't hurt.

In the meantime, there's a velvet rope hammock strung between the last old maples in the row. Roy's hand is in mine and the heat rises from the nearby fields, bringing us the stir of an evening breeze. We're slung like lovebirds a few feet above the ground.

•   •   •

IN RECOGNITION

Versions of these stories have appeared
in the following publications.

A Father's Will: *Groundswell* Vol. 1, No. 2

A Language of the Soul: *Prairie Winds* 2004

Close to the Earth: *Riversedge* Vol. XV, No. 1

Family Trust: *Limestone* 2007

In the Game: *Red Rock Review* Vol. 1, no. 8

Natural Causes: *Cimarron Review* No. 142

Signs: *WLA--War, Literature and Art* (USAFA) 2008
and *Studio One: Spring 2008*

The Florida Room: *RE:AL* Vol. XXIV

Voices Along the Road: *Readers Break* Vol. VIII and *ELM
(Eureka Literary Magazine)* Vol. 10, No. 1

ACCLAIM

"Gary McLouth is a rare writer in how he champions the appearance of truth and goodness in everyone as it rises forth in the most ordinary of circumstances. He never denies the hardships that life on earth presents, but somehow with a clear heart and wide eye shows us that an angel waits inside each of us for the darkest time to rise; not with choirs or white wings, but with sweat and effort and small indispensable kindnesses. These stories will help you get out of bed in the morning."

– Mark Nepo, author of *Surviving Has Made Me Crazy* and *Facing the Lion, Being the Lion*

"The short stories in *Natural Causes* so capture these people and their 'rituals'. The pleasure and insight of the stories haunt me.

– Ginny Howsam, western New York native

"If a fiction writer's job is to observe the world closely, to think clearly about what he has seen, and then to transmute those considered observations into a fictional world that readers feel compelled to enter, experience, and enjoy, then Gary McLouth, in his new collection, Natural Causes and other stories, has more than done his job."

– William Patrick, author of *Saving Troy*

"Gary McLouth's stories are grounded in the middle decades of the 20th century in western New York's hinterlands, an era and a place long vanished. The simple, honest folk who inhabit these pages and their timeless dramas of love and loss manage to evoke universal truths for us all."

– Paul Grondahl, author of *Mayor Corning: Albany Icon, Albany Enigma* and *I Rose Like a Rocket: The Political Education of Theodore Roosevelt*

"Gary McLouth writes so convincingly about the people of upstate New York that even if you've never visited the place you come away feeling you grew up there. Above all, the stories in *Natural Causes* are moving and authentic. You've met these characters, you've talked with them, you may have even gossiped about their misadventures."

– Eugene Mirabelli, author of *The Goddess in Love with a Horse*

"I know these people, thank goodness. I grew up with them in Western New York, they're my friends and my friends' parents, and now I know some of their secrets, thoughts, fears and dreams I couldn't have ever known before. Gary McLouth has brought this world back, and forward."

– Jeanne Finley, writer and editor, New York native

"The stories in Natural Causes are rich with the rhythms and rituals of rural life. Here in western New York State, seasons turn slowly. Winter lasts more than half the year. So the people in these stories take comfort in being inside—inside their houses; inside their barns and garages; and, most important, inside the circle of family. Gary McLouth portrays the Wells family in all its complexity—Doc Wells, the country practitioner; his wife; his two daughters; and his son come to full life and being here. Each member of the family serves as a narrator for a story. Singly, each voice is compelling; together, the voices weave an intricate web of kinship. Family life is not idealized or sentimentalized, but still the reader feels its power. We, too, long to be insiders and McLouth's stories allow us that pleasure.

"*Natural Causes*, like a good map, is knit together by miles and miles of rural road. In this kind of country, people spend much of their lives on the road. Newly licensed teenagers feel the exhilaration of freedom, workers commute, a doctor makes his daily rounds, a son comes home to visit. Everyone knows that around any curve, at any moment, instant disaster waits: a leaping deer, a patch of ice, a drunk driver crossing the center line. Roads, like families, are where life and death happen. And roads lend themselves to reflection. As Doc Wells muses, "You get to run your life by in little scenes and snippets while you're out driving between one thing and another." The stories, scenes and snippets in *Natural Causes* will stay with you for a long time. Gary McLouth is a great driver; let him take you for a memorable ride in the countryside he knows so well."

– *Hollis Seamon, author of* Body Work: Stories *and*
Flesh: A Suzanne LaFleshe Mystery